Caught!

Kit held her breath, wondering if the woman would notice that the bracelet was missing. She didn't.

Kit tried to act casual. "I'd better go," she said to Marcia.

"See you at rehearsal," Marcia said.

Over my dead body, Kit thought, but she forced a smile before she turned and walked away.

As she rode up the escalator, she kept her hand in her pocket, fingering the bracelet.

A new thought hit her. What if the store had secret cameras hidden? Panicky, she scrutinized the ceiling and the walls above each sales counter. She saw nothing that resembled a camera.

Kit felt hot. She needed to get out of the mall. She didn't want to call attention to herself by running but she walked quickly, as if she were late for an appointment.

As she stepped out into the main corridor of the mall, someone touched her elbow.

The woman held a small black folder toward Kit. She flipped the folder open.

There was a badge inside.

"I'm with store security."

• ᴖ •

"Kit's determination to free herself from the cages of . . . jealousy and ultimately, the secret of her crime make her an appealing protagonist."

—*School Library Journal*

Cages

PEG KEHRET

SCHOLASTIC INC.

New York Toronto London Auckland Sydney
Mexico City New Delhi Hong Kong Buenos Aires

ISBN 0-439-42217-5

Copyright © 1991 by Peg Kehret.
All rights reserved.
Published by Scholastic Inc., 557 Broadway, New York, NY 10012, by arrangement with Puffin Books, a member of Penguin Putnam Inc.
SCHOLASTIC and associated logos are trademarks and/or registered trademarks of Scholastic Inc.

12 11 10 9 8 7 6 5 4 3 2   2 3 4 5 6 7/0

Printed in the U.S.A.   40

First Scholastic printing, July 2002

Cages

CHAPTER 1

IT was almost over. Kit Hathaway glanced at her notecards, but her hands shook so badly that she couldn't read her own writing.

This was her last and most important speech of the year, the one that would determine her final grade, although that wasn't why she was nervous. It was her topic. Of all the subjects in the world, why did she have to get this one for her final speech?

Her closing statement rushed out. "If you're caught shoplifting," she said, "your parents are notified, and the police come, and the juvenile court decides your punishment. It's stupid to take such a chance."

She nodded to Miss Fenton, indicating that she was finished. At last. Feeling drained of energy, she started back to her seat.

Before she got there, a boy in the back of the room said, "That's a bunch of bull."

Kit stopped.

"Do you wish to challenge this speech, Arthur?" Miss Fenton said.

"Yes," he said. "Yes, I challenge it. Hardly anybody gets caught. Not if they're careful. I know lots of guys who take stuff all the time and not one of them has ever been busted."

Kit hesitated. Her classmates watched her, alert, awaiting her response. If she didn't defend her position, it was an automatic drop of one full grade. But how could she prove her point without divulging her secret?

None of the other kids knew. Not even her best friend, Tracy. And Kit intended to keep it that way.

"A buddy of mine takes a candy bar from the Ben Franklin store every day after school," Arthur said. "Every day. He's done it since we were in kindergarten and he's never been caught once."

Kit glared at Arthur. Why couldn't he keep his big mouth shut? He's probably the one who swipes a candy bar every day, not his buddy.

"Kit?" Miss Fenton said.

Kit's throat felt tight.

A new voice spoke up. This time, it was Arthur's buddy, Phil. "Arthur's right," he said. "Lots of kids shoplift and hardly anyone ever gets caught. Even if you do, they let you off easy the first time. You don't have to go to jail or anything."

Kit clenched her teeth. What was this, National Gang-Up-on-Kit Week? Was everybody in the whole class going to try to raise their grade by challenging Kit's speech?

2

They made it sound so simple. Nothing to it. Just walk into the Ben Franklin, day after day, and help yourself to a candy bar. No problem.

Only it didn't always work that way.

Arthur's voice grew louder. "Kit quoted a bunch of statistics," he said, "but statistics aren't real life. I've had experience and I say Kit's wrong."

Kit felt someone nudge her in the ribs. Turning, she saw that she was standing beside Tracy's desk. Tracy held a note-card so Kit could see what it said. "BRILLIANT SPEAKER STUNS CLASS WITH STATISTICS; HECKLERS SILENCED FOREVER."

Months earlier, Kit and Tracy had gone into fits of laughter at the supermarket, over the headlines of a tabloid newspaper. "Four-year-old Gives Birth to Lizard," it had said, and, "Embalmed Body Rises from Grave to Accuse Ex-husband of Murder!!"

Ever since, Kit and Tracy had written exaggerated headlines for each other and joked about their future careers as Sharon Shocker and Harriet Headline, raunchy reporters.

Kit smiled weakly at Tracy. Tracy put the sign down and nodded encouragingly. Kit knew Tracy wanted her to defend her speech. Meet Arthur's challenge. Put him in his place.

Oh, Tracy, she thought. You don't know what you're asking of me.

She could do it, if she wanted to. She could prove that she was right. She could zap Arthur with information that would stun him into silence.

All she had to do was tell the class what had happened to her. Tell them about the fear and the guilt and the lies. Tell them about the shame and the tears.

I can't do it, Kit thought. I don't want them to know. Not now. Not ever.

Tracy nudged her again and whispered, "Do it."

Kit felt trapped. If she defended her speech, everyone would know her secret. If she sat down now, what would she say to Tracy? How could she explain?

Miss Fenton spoke quietly. "Do you want to defend your speech, Kit? This minute is passing."

It was, Kit knew, a line from the play. ". . . while we're talking right now, this minute is passing."

This minute is passing. The quote swept Kit back in time, back to the day when the cast list was posted.

The day her life was changed forever.

The day her secret began.

CHAPTER

2

ON the day the cast list was posted, Kit had been too excited to eat breakfast. Although she knew the list would not be there until classes ended, she left early for school.

"Don't get your hopes up too high," her mother warned. "Sometimes the things we look forward to the most turn out to be the biggest disappointments."

Kit didn't answer. She had a chance. Not just for a small part, a chance for the lead. Frankie.

Kit knew she was being considered for the part. Why else would Miss Fenton ask her to read Frankie's lines more than once?

In her mind, Kit saw the program: "The Drama Department of Kennedy School presents *The Member of the Wedding* by Carson McCullers, starring Kit Hathaway as Frankie."

Kit could already see herself on stage, could hear the audience laugh when she spoke Frankie's lines: "Oh, I am so worried about being tall. I'm twelve and five-sixths years old and already five feet five and three-fourths inches tall. If I keep on growing like this until I'm twenty-one, I figure I will be nearly ten feet tall."

Kit was five feet five and three-fourths inches tall. Exactly. She thought it was a good omen. Of course, she was already fourteen, but her brown hair was long and when she braided it, she looked younger. For once, she was glad she had a thin, boyish figure. With the right clothes, she could easily pass for "twelve and five-sixths."

She could almost hear the standing ovation.

If she got the part of Frankie and did a good job with it, she might even get the Ninth Grade Scholarship. It was awarded at the end of the school year on the basis of scholarship and extracurricular activities. Kit's grades were high enough to qualify but she wasn't inclined to join clubs. She liked books better than crowds and felt shy with people she didn't know well. She and Tracy cheered at all the school football and volleyball games but spectators don't win scholarships. You have to participate.

She knew she had to earn a scholarship if she hoped to attend college. Wayne wouldn't pay any tuition, that was certain. Her stepfather thought college was a waste of time.

"Why do you need a degree?" he had asked, the first time Kit mentioned college. "What do you want to do?"

Kit admitted that she didn't know yet what field she wanted to enter.

"Why spend four years paying to go to school," he said,

"when you could work those four years and have someone pay you?"

One thing at a time, Kit thought. College is three years away. Get the part of Frankie first, then worry about the scholarship.

If she got the part, she planned to surprise Miss Fenton by knowing her lines quickly. She had already memorized the whole first act. For days, she and Tracy had quoted lines to each other, working them into their conversation whenever possible and waiting to see if the other person caught on.

Kit's favorite line was, "I feel just exactly like somebody has peeled all the skin off me." So far, she had not been able to fit that one into any conversation.

"Let's make a deal," Tracy said, on the day that the cast list was to be posted. "If one of us gets a part and the other doesn't, the one who doesn't will help backstage. That way, we both work on the play, no matter what."

"Agreed," Kit said. She hoped Tracy would get a part but she knew Tracy would have just as much fun helping with props or costumes. Tracy was like that. She could accept whatever happened and be happy. Kit's mother often suggested that Kit should be more like Tracy.

As soon as the final bell rang, signaling the end of sixth period, Kit and Tracy hurried to the school's auditorium. There was already a crowd of people around the list, jostling each other impatiently and craning their necks, trying to see which names were on it.

Kit felt a knot in the pit of her stomach. *Please,* she thought. *Please, please let me be Frankie. I know I can do it. All I need is a chance to prove it.*

At the front of the crowd, someone shrieked, "I got it! I got

Janice!" Congratulations from the shrieker's friends mingled with groans of disappointment from other would-be actresses who had read for the part of Janice.

At last, Kit was close enough to read the list. The names of the characters were on the left side of the paper. Opposite each, on the right side, was the name of the student who would be playing that role.

Kit's eyes skimmed quickly down the right-hand list, looking for Kit Hathaway. Almost at the bottom, she spotted Tracy Shelburn.

Tracy saw it at the same time. "I got a part," Tracy said. She sounded amazed. "Look, Kit. I'm going to be Doris."

Kit didn't answer right away. She was reading the list again, hoping she'd made a mistake the first time.

There was no mistake. Her name wasn't there.

She forced herself to smile at Tracy. "Congratulations," she said. "You'll be a great Doris."

"It isn't a very big part," Tracy said. "I'll have plenty of time to be backstage with you."

Kit looked one more time at the list. She had to know who got the part she'd wanted.

"Oh, no," Kit said. She whispered to Tracy, "Marcia Homer's going to be Frankie."

Tracy groaned, rolling her eyes. "Miss Fenton must be temporarily insane," she said.

"I can't stand it," Kit said. "Anybody but her."

Because their last names both started with *H*, Kit and Marcia were often assigned seats beside each other. Marcia's father gave her twenty dollars for every *A* she got on her report card and Marcia never failed to tell Kit about it. Once, when Marcia got five *A*s, her father actually gave her a one-hundred-dollar bill. Still, it wasn't Marcia's money that bothered Kit, it was her constant chatter about herself. Yak yak yak. Me, me, me. Endlessly. How could Miss Fenton have chosen Marcia to play the part of Frankie?

Kit turned away in disgust. She no longer wanted to help backstage. She didn't want anything to do with *The Member of the Wedding*.

"Come on," Tracy said, as she tugged on Kit's sleeve. "Let's go to the meeting."

Reluctantly, Kit followed Tracy down the hall to Miss Fenton's classroom, where all cast members and anyone who wanted to work on the production crew were supposed to meet. She wished she had not agreed to Tracy's deal. All she wanted to do was go home. She needed to be alone for awhile.

When they got to the meeting, Marcia was already there. Kit managed to avoid looking at her but it was impossible not to hear her.

"I am absolutely thrilled to death," Marcia gushed. "I never dreamed I'd get the lead. I mean, I wanted it, of course—didn't we all?—but I just never thought I'd really be the one to actually get it. I called my parents right away and they're absolutely thrilled to death, too."

I hope she forgets her lines on opening night, Kit thought. I hope she falls on her face and makes a fool of herself.

She handed Tracy a note. "DRAMA COACH FLINGS ACTRESS OFF CLIFF AFTER FIRST REHEARSAL."

Moments later, the note came back. Tracy had added: "MILLIONS CHEER."

When Miss Fenton asked for volunteers for the various pro-

9

duction committees, Kit did not raise her hand. She couldn't stand to think of working backstage and listening to Marcia say Frankie's lines every day. On the other hand, she had made a pact with Tracy and she didn't want to let Tracy down. It wasn't Tracy's fault that Miss Fenton cast Marcia in the lead role. Finally, Kit agreed to make posters and put them up. She could do that at home, where she didn't have to listen to Marcia.

"Do you want me to bring you some studio photos of myself for the posters?" Marcia asked.

"That won't be necessary," Miss Fenton said. "Any photos we use for advertising will be taken during rehearsals."

And, Kit thought, the ones I use will not be of you, Motormouth. She would ask the photographer to shoot the scene where Doris appears. Why not give Tracy the glory?

As they left the meeting, Tracy said, "I'll give you my candy opinion. Marcia will drive us all nuts before this is over."

"Candy opinion" was a phrase from the play but this time, Kit didn't respond. The game of quoting lines wasn't fun anymore. Not now. Losing the role of Frankie, especially to Marcia Homer, hurt too much.

"Do something nice for yourself when you get home," Tracy said, as they left the school. "It would be a good night for the Triple-B Treatment."

For the first time since she'd read the list of cast members, Kit smiled. Leave it to Tracy to suggest the one thing in the world that would make her feel better.

"See you tomorrow," Tracy said.

"I'm glad you got a part," Kit said.

She *was* glad for Tracy but as she walked home, her own disappointment stuck in her throat. She'd tried so hard and she felt she'd read the lines as well as she was capable of reading them. That's what hurt the most. She'd given it her best shot and her best wasn't good enough. There was no standing ovation in her future now; there was only the thankless task of making posters.

Well, there was no point crying about it. Maybe she'd take Tracy's advice. Treat herself to the Triple-B. She opened her purse and looked to see if she had enough money to buy a bag of chocolate stars.

The Triple-B Treatment consisted of three things: 1. a long, hot bubble bath 2. a good book to read 3. a bag of chocolate stars. Bath, book, and bag of candy: all three at the same time. She would lock herself in the bathroom, fill the tub with bubbles, place the bag of candy on the edge of the tub, and climb in. Then she'd lie in the warm water, read her book, and eat the chocolate. There was even a ritual about how she ate the chocolate stars: slowly, one at a time. She never took a bite; she only sucked, letting each one melt completely before she took another.

Nobody but Tracy knew about the Triple-B Treatment, not even Kit's mother. Especially not Kit's mother.

She stopped at the 7-Eleven on her way home and bought the chocolate stars, hiding them in the bottom of her bookbag, underneath her math homework, where her mother wouldn't see them.

Dorothy Gillette didn't allow candy in the house. "It only makes people fat," she declared. In Dorothy's view, being fat was an inexcusable crime that should be punishable by law. She ran six miles every afternoon, to ensure that the enemy didn't creep onto her hips when she wasn't looking.

Dorothy was trim, no doubt about that. If only she didn't feel so superior to anyone who wasn't. Kit preferred Miss Fenton's attitude. Miss Fenton laughed at her own pudgy figure and admitted, "Doughnuts are my downfall. Especially chocolate-frosted ones."

A bath, a book, and a bag of chocolate. Kit felt better already, anticipating the Triple-B.

As she approached her house, she saw Wayne's car in the driveway. Why was he home so early? Her stepfather never got home before 6:30 and it wasn't yet 5:00. Usually he put his car in the garage. Maybe Wayne was sick. Or maybe— Kit's mouth felt dry. Maybe he was on another binge.

She approached the house cautiously, listening. Wayne got drunk every four or five months. When he did, he was surly, often shouting and throwing things. His binges lasted for several days, during which Kit's mother tiptoed around the house, cleaning up the messes Wayne made and trying to calm him down.

Once Kit had suggested that Wayne should get help for his drinking problem.

"Wayne doesn't have a drinking problem," Dorothy said. "He only drinks two or three times a year."

Kit didn't know if Wayne was an alcoholic or not. All she knew was that when he went on one of his binges, life at home was miserable.

She eased the front door open. Silence. She stepped inside.

Maybe he was sick. The flu was going around. Maybe Wayne had the flu.

She hung her coat in the closet and headed for her bedroom. Before she got there, she heard Wayne shout from the kitchen.

"Damn it, Dorothy," Wayne yelled. "You know I don't like broiled salmon. Why are you fixing salmon for dinner when you know I don't like it?"

Kit stopped. She knew that tone of voice all too well. She also knew that Wayne had never mentioned a dislike for salmon. He had, in fact, always eaten salmon with gusto.

Kit listened.

"I'm sorry," Dorothy said. "I won't fix salmon again. Now, what would you like instead? I'll just run out to the grocery store and buy something else."

Kit clenched her teeth. She hated it when her mother let Wayne doormat her like that. Anything to keep the peace, Dorothy always said, but Kit never felt peace was achieved. It was more like surrender.

Crash! A loud noise exploded from the kitchen. Kit jumped. Then she hurried into the kitchen to see what had happened. Her mother stood beside the stove, blotting her blue sweatsuit with a dish towel. Wayne sat at the kitchen table, barefoot, wearing a suit and tie.

Amber liquid trickled down the front of the refrigerator and dripped into pieces of broken glass on the tile floor. Kit inhaled the strong, sharp smell of liquor.

"My glass slipped," Wayne said.

"It certainly did," Dorothy said, as she got a broom and started sweeping up the shards of glass.

"Slipped right out of my hand," Wayne said.

Kit said nothing.

"Don't just stand there," Wayne said. "Your mother needs help with this mess."

Kit glared at him.

"Never mind," Dorothy said. "I'll clean it up."

Kit turned and started to leave the kitchen.

"Kit!" Wayne shouted. "You stay here and wash off the refrigerator."

Kit wanted to scream. First she wasn't cast in the play, then she'd had to listen to Mouthy Marcia, and now Wayne was on another binge.

"Wash it off yourself," she said. "You're the one who threw your glass and made a mess. Why should we clean it up for you?"

"She doesn't mean that, Wayne," Dorothy said. "We know it was an accident."

Just once, Kit thought. Just once, why can't you stick up for me? Why must you always pretend he's sober?

"It wasn't an accident," Kit said. "He's drunk and he threw his glass on purpose. Why can't you admit that?"

Dorothy winced. "Please," she said, "don't make things worse."

"You animal," Wayne said. He stood up and pounded his fist on the table. "That's what you are. Nothing but a stupid little animal."

"Now, Wayne," Dorothy said. "You don't mean that. He doesn't mean that, Kit."

He had called her that before when he was drunk and it

14

always made her furious. Kit spun around and rushed out of the kitchen. Wayne lurched after her.

She wasn't afraid of him. Although Wayne bellowed and called her names when he was drunk, he had never hit her nor, to her knowledge, had he ever hit her mother. But Kit refused to listen to any more. She grabbed her coat, picked up her bookbag, and ran outside, slamming the door behind her.

As she sprinted down the sidewalk, she heard Wayne open the door and shout after her. With no walls to confine it, his voice seemed louder and deeper. The harsh words chased her, nipping at her heels.

"Animal!"

"Animal."

"Animal. . . ."

CHAPTER
3

THE bus wheezed to a stop. Kit looked out the window. Should she get off here or ride a few more blocks?

She decided to keep riding, all the way to the mall. The mall was open until nine; she would wander through the stores until then. Maybe she would try on some clothes, daydream a little before she went back home.

She knew she would go home. Although Kit sometimes fantasized about running away, she had no place to go. Despite her problems, she knew she was better off at home than on the street. Most of the time Wayne was OK—not great but tolerable. His binges always made life miserable for awhile but she knew from experience that in a few days, Wayne would be sober and contrite, swearing to Kit's mother that he would never drink like that again. Never. And Dorothy always seemed to believe him.

Kit got off the bus at the main entrance to the mall and went inside. The aroma of melted cheese, sausage, and tomato sauce floated from Pizza Hut. Her stomach growled. She wished she had some of the broiled salmon that Wayne was so angry about. At noon, Kit had been too excited and nervous about the cast list to eat lunch and she'd spent all but twenty-three cents of her money on the bag of chocolate stars and bus fare. She couldn't even buy herself a sandwich.

Mentally, she became Sharon Shocker. "EMACIATED BODY FOUND IN MALL. STUDENT STARVES IN FRONT OF PIZZA HUT."

She sat on one of the benches in the center of the mall, opened the bag of candy, and popped a chocolate star in her mouth. She rolled the candy around with her tongue, making it melt. It wasn't as good as the Triple-B Treatment but it was the best she could do.

The mall was crowded. Shoppers hurried past, laughing and talking. Surrounded by people, Kit felt completely alone. Everyone else in the world seemed to have someplace to go and someone to talk to.

The longer she sat there, the more miserable she felt. It wasn't fair. She would have been a good Frankie. Better than Marcia the Mouth. And Marcia could afford to go to college without a scholarship.

She ate some more chocolate stars. Why should she have to put up with Wayne's insults, just because Wayne got drunk and Dorothy wouldn't stand up to him? Why did he always have to call her an animal? He's the one who acted less than human, not her.

17

She ate another chocolate star. If her face broke out tomorrow, what difference did it make? Who would care?

Tears filled her eyes. Kit stood up, wiped her eyes on the back of her hand, and jammed the remaining chocolate stars into her bookbag. Then she headed for Pierre's. Maybe she'd feel better if she tried on the latest fashions. Kit couldn't afford to buy anything, but there was no charge for looking.

She lingered awhile on the main floor, listening to the music. A shiny black grand piano stood beside the escalators, while the pianist, in black suit and black bow tie, sent elegant music up and down the moving stairs.

She rode the escalator down, intending to try some free cosmetic samples. As she passed through the jewelry department, she heard someone call out, "Kit."

Marcia Homer stood a few yards away, waving. "Kit!" she called again. "Come here a minute."

Kit walked over to where Marcia stood with a salesclerk and a stocky man in a dark overcoat.

"Daddy," Marcia said, "this is Kit Hathaway. She's going to do the publicity for my play. Look, Kit, Daddy's buying me a present, to celebrate my getting the lead."

Kit didn't want to look but she knew it would be rude not to. Mr. Homer beamed as the salesclerk pointed to several pieces of gold jewelry.

"I get my choice," Marcia said. "Isn't it exciting? They're all 24-carat gold and I can have whichever one I want. Which would you pick, Kit? Help me decide."

The clerk put another box, containing a locket, on top of the glass-topped counter.

Kit looked at the glittering array. Each box was lined with soft gray velvet; each held a piece of jewelry. Some boxes contained more than one piece. The treasures sparkled and gleamed like a pirate's bounty.

The largest box held bracelets. Kit eyed them longingly. One was particularly beautiful. It was made of three slender strands of gold, braided together. If Kit had her choice, she'd take the braided gold bracelet but she didn't tell Marcia that.

"They're all pretty," she said.

"I kind of like that thick gold choker," Marcia said. She giggled. "It looks the most expensive."

Kit thought the choker was gaudy but she said nothing. Mr. Homer picked up the choker; the clerk held Marcia's hair up while Mr. Homer fastened the choker around Marcia's neck.

Watching them, Kit felt even more alone than she had earlier. Kit's father had died when Kit was four. She still kept his picture on the table beside her bed but when she looked at it, he seemed more like a character in a book than someone she had known and loved and lived with.

Her only real memory of him was of sitting on his lap each evening, snuggling close while he read the comic section of the newspaper out loud. She could not remember his voice or his laugh; she remembered only that she was happy when he read to her. She did not remember how he looked, either, except for that brief moment in time when the camera captured him. When she closed her eyes, she could remember the photograph, but not the man.

Kit was nine when her mother married Wayne Gillette. By then she could read the comics herself.

Two weeks after the wedding, Wayne got drunk. Kit was shocked by his loud, rude ways and horrified by her mother's docile acceptance of them.

During that first binge, Wayne told Kit it was time to stop calling him Mr. Gillette and start calling him Dad.

Kit shook her head.

"You don't want to call me Dad?"

She shook her head again.

"Fine. You can call me Father." Wayne laughed uproariously. "That's even better. I'm your father now; that's what you should call me. Father."

Loathing rose in Kit as she looked at the unshaven, disheveled man. "You aren't my father," she said. "You'll never be my father."

The laughter stopped abruptly.

Kit's mother, too quickly, said, "She doesn't mean that, Wayne."

"Yes, I do," Kit said.

"Please don't be difficult," her mother said. "Wayne is your stepfather now; it's only natural to call him Dad."

Kit couldn't believe that her own mother would betray her.

"Before long, you'll *want* to call him Dad," her mother went on. "Until then, you must do it because it's important to Wayne. And to me."

Kit never did it. She just didn't call him anything. And from that day on, she never again called her mother, Mom. It was always Dorothy.

At first, Dorothy asked her not to. "I'm your mother. I want to be called Mom, not Dorothy." When Kit persisted, Dorothy gave up.

20

Kit often wondered what her life would be like if her father had lived.

Marcia and Mr. Homer blurred; Kit blinked furiously, angry at herself for being so emotional.

"Oh, this is so elegant," Marcia said. "Real gold against my skin makes me feel like a queen." She put both hands to her throat and stroked the choker. "How does it look on me?"

"See for yourself," the clerk said. She turned an oval mirror, which sat on the countertop, toward Marcia. Marcia peered at herself while the clerk gradually adjusted the mirror to give Marcia a view from a different angle. Mr. Homer hovered behind Marcia like a bee at an apple blossom.

Kit looked longingly at the slender braided bracelet. No one ever bought her a present of any kind unless it was her birthday and even then she never got anything like this. Dorothy believed in practical gifts. Pantyhose. Knit gloves. Hand lotion.

Kit wondered how the bracelet would look on her arm. She picked it up and draped it across her wrist. It was even more beautiful up close. She stepped nearer to the light on the counter, and moved her arm back and forth, watching the bracelet glint and shine.

The clerk said, "The choker makes you look older. More sophisticated." Marcia admired herself and Mr. Homer admired Marcia. No one paid any attention to Kit.

She hated them. All of them. She hated Marcia for getting the part of Frankie and she hated Mr. Homer for spoiling his daughter rotten and she hated the clerk for fawning over them, trying to make a big sale. She hated Wayne for getting drunk and yelling at her and she hated her mother for letting him get away with it. At that moment, Kit hated the whole world.

21

She took the bracelet off her wrist and held it in her hand. She thought of a line from the play: "All my life I've been wantin' things that I ain't been gettin'." As the rage boiled up inside her, she decided not to put the bracelet back on the tray. She would keep it.

She looked quickly over both shoulders. Except for two young women who stood one aisle over, discussing some purses that were on sale, there was no one around.

Kit swallowed hard, and glanced again at Marcia, Mr. Homer, and the clerk. They were still ignoring her. In the distance, the piano music grew louder. This minute is passing, she thought. If I'm going to do it, it has to be now.

Quickly, she shoved the gold bracelet in the pocket of her coat.

She looked around again. Had anyone seen her? The two women were still discussing the purses, Marcia was still turning her head from side to side, and the clerk was agreeing with Mr. Homer that Marcia was a beautiful young woman.

Kit stood perfectly still. Her heart raced and she could feel the blood rush to her face but nobody noticed. She might as well have been a store mannequin.

The piano notes floated in the air. Marcia chattered on about the gold choker while the patient saleswoman adjusted the mirror one more time.

Kit stepped slightly to her right, lifted a gold locket from its box and examined it. She put the locket back and briefly inspected a lapel pin.

She flexed her fingers, as if to prove to anyone who might be watching that her hands were empty. Then she put her hand in her pocket and closed her fingers around the bracelet. She could still put the bracelet back, if she wanted to. All she had to do was take it out of her pocket and put it on the tray and no one would ever know she'd removed it in the first place.

But she didn't. Somehow, that gold bracelet now symbolized everything she had ever wanted and couldn't have: a father who didn't die, a mother who understood her, a part in the school play.

Just this once, she thought. I'll never steal anything again but just this once I'm going to have what I want. I will keep this bracelet. I'll hide it in my underwear drawer and when my birthday comes, I'll wear it to school and show it to Marcia and tell her it's a gift from my mother. I deserve it! Why should Marcia be the only one to have gold jewelry? And Pierre's won't go bankrupt over one little bracelet.

"Kit."

Kit jumped when Marcia spoke, as if the other girl could read her thoughts. "I've decided," Marcia said. "This choker is the one I want."

"We'll take it," Mr. Homer said.

"I'll wear it home," Marcia said.

The clerk wrote up the sale and took Mr. Homer's money before she remembered to put the other boxes of jewelry back inside the glass case.

Kit held her breath, wondering if the woman would notice that the bracelet was missing. She didn't. She was talking to Mr. Homer, asking if he wanted to open a charge account.

Kit tried to act casual. "I'd better go," she said to Marcia.

"See you at rehearsal," Marcia said.

Over my dead body, Kit thought, but she forced a smile before she turned and walked away.

23

As she rode up the escalator, she kept her hand in her pocket, fingering the bracelet.

A new thought hit her. TV monitors. What if the store had secret cameras hidden and someone in a control room watched all the monitors to see if anyone was shoplifting? Panicky, she scrutinized the ceiling and the walls above each sales counter. She saw nothing that resembled a camera.

Kit felt hot. She swallowed and started for the exit. She needed to get out of the mall. Get outside and breathe some fresh air. She didn't want to call attention to herself by running but she walked quickly, as if she were late for an appointment.

As she stepped out into the main corridor of the mall, someone touched her elbow.

Turning, Kit saw one of the women who had been trying to decide which purse to buy.

The woman held a small black folder toward Kit. She flipped the folder open.

There was a badge inside.

"I'm with store security," the woman said softly. "I'd like you to come to the office with me to discuss some missing merchandise."

Kit stood stone still. She thought security guards wore uniforms. This woman wore a black miniskirt and a pink print shirt and open-toed shoes with high heels. But the badge was authentic and the look in the woman's eyes told Kit that she was authentic, too.

Kit wished that the floor of the mall would suddenly open and let her drop out of sight. She wished the piano player would strike a mighty chord that would send her magically up the escalator and out through the ceiling. She wished a fire would break out and everyone would have to run outside and the smoke would be so thick, she could slip away unseen.

"This way," the woman said.

Perspiration trickled down Kit's arms. The chocolate stars which had melted so gently on her tongue now threatened to erupt violently from her stomach.

How could I have been such a fool? she thought. I don't need a gold bracelet and I sure don't need to get picked up for shoplifting. What would her mother say? And Wayne. Wayne would never let her forget it.

Maybe the store would let her go with only a warning. It was her first time, after all. She had no record; she'd never been in any trouble. Maybe the store would go easy on her and her mother would never find out.

She remembered seeing signs in the past that said, "Shoplifters Will Be Prosecuted." Had she seen such a sign in Pierre's? She couldn't remember.

The woman said nothing more. As they walked, Kit felt conspicuous, like a giant spotlight was on her. When they went through the jewelry section, the clerk who had waited on Mr. Homer and Marcia looked over at Kit and smiled. Then she saw who Kit was with. She frowned and quickly checked the boxes of gold jewelry which had been out on the counter. The next time she looked at Kit, she didn't smile. Kit's cheeks burned and she walked faster, staring at the floor. She would never be able to come into Pierre's again.

Her coat felt invisible; the bracelet, deep in her pocket, must be obvious to anyone who looked.

Why had she thought she could get away with it? How could she have been so stupid? She could just hear Marcia, telling everyone how Kit had been so envious of her new gold choker that she stole some jewelry for herself. Marcia would embellish the story to make herself the only reason Kit had taken the bracelet.

She wished a bolt of lightning would strike her dead before they got to the office.

"Here we are," the woman said, as she held a door open. Kit took a deep breath and went in.

CHAPTER
4

DO you know why you're here?"

The security officer put her arms on her desk and leaned toward Kit, watching her intently.

Kit stared down at her lap. Maybe she could still bluff her way out of this. "No," she said. Her voice sounded shaky and she pressed her lips together, trying to get control of herself.

"You are here," the woman said, "because you were seen shoplifting."

Kit's head jerked up.

"You can either tell the truth and we'll do this the easy way," the woman said, "or you can refuse to cooperate, deny everything, and we'll do it the hard way." She paused a moment. "Now, I'd like you to give me the merchandise you took."

Kit hesitated. What did the woman mean when she said they could do it the hard way? She decided not to find out. She slipped her hand in her coat pocket, pulled out the gold bracelet, and dropped it on the woman's desk.

The woman reached for the telephone. "I'll call your parents," she said. "What's the number?"

Kit told her.

"Are they both at that number?"

"My mother is. And my stepfather."

"What's your mother's name?"

"Dorothy Gillette. But do you have to call her?" Kit leaned forward, her hands gripping the arms of the chair. "I've never taken anything before and I swear I'll never do it again."

"I have to call," the woman said, as she punched the numbers.

Kit closed her eyes. That was it, then. Her mother would find out and so would Wayne. Probably the whole school would know, even Tracy and Miss Fenton. Any faint chance she might have had for the Ninth Grade Scholarship had just blown out the window.

The woman said, "Mrs. Gillette? This is Hannah Rydecker. I'm with the security department of Pierre's. Your daughter was shoplifting and I would like you to come down to the store and get her."

Kit listened while the woman told Dorothy where to come. After she hung up, she said, "Your mother is on her way. We'll release you to her custody until the Juvenile Court decides how to proceed."

Kit wanted to run. She wished she could dig a hole and crawl in it and hide. She didn't want to go to Juvenile Court.

She didn't want to be guilty of shoplifting. Most of all she didn't want to see the look on her mother's face when Dorothy got to Pierre's.

There was no way to run and no place to hide. Frankie's line from the play popped into her mind. "I feel just exactly like somebody has peeled all the skin off me."

Kit slumped in her chair and waited.

The woman began writing, filling out some kind of form. "What's your name?" she asked.

"Kit Hathaway."

The woman wrote it on the form.

"Age?"

"Fourteen."

"Is this shoplifting incident related to any drug problem?"

"No." Why would she think that?

Mrs. Rydecker seemed to believe her. "A lot of shoplifting is drug related," she said, as she continued to write on the form. She leaned back in her chair. "A police officer will be here soon. He'll have other questions for you."

Kit wiped the palms of her hands on her jeans. The walls of the office seemed to be closing in on her. Feeling trapped and helpless, and far more scared than she'd ever been before, she fought to hold back the tears.

The officer who arrived was in uniform. The name plate above his badge said, "Sergeant Adams."

The woman handed him the form she had filled out and he read it quickly.

"Have you mirandized her yet?" he asked the woman.

"No."

The officer stood beside Kit and spoke rapidly. "You have

the right to remain silent," he said. "Anything you say can and will be used against you in court. You have the right to consult with a lawyer and to have a lawyer with you during this interrogation. If you are indigent, a lawyer will be appointed to represent you."

Kit could see no point in remaining silent and she didn't think a lawyer would help. She had already admitted her guilt by giving the bracelet back. The woman had said it would be easier for her if she told the truth and that's what she planned to do.

"Are the statements in this report true?" Sergeant Adams showed Kit the form that Mrs. Rydecker had given him.

"Yes."

"You are under arrest for shoplifting."

"Under arrest? But I gave the bracelet back. I told the truth and I thought . . ."

Sergeant Adams interrupted. "Did you take the bracelet?" he asked.

"Yes."

"Why?"

Kit shrugged.

"Did you need money for drugs?"

"No." Why did they keep asking her if she was on drugs? Did she look like an addict?

"Do you have a problem at home?" Mrs. Rydecker asked.

Kit looked at her. Mrs. Rydecker smiled. Kit shook her head.

"No trouble with your folks?"

Kit thought about Wayne. She remembered him yelling after her, "Animal!" But she didn't want to talk about that. Certainly not with strangers.

"Sometimes people shoplift because they have problems they can't cope with," Mrs. Rydecker said. "If that's the case with you, you can tell us about it and we'll try to help."

Kit shook her head again. She didn't want any social worker coming around, poking into her family's personal business. By the time someone got there, Wayne would be sober and he and Dorothy would deny that there was any problem and Kit would be in a worse mess than she was already in.

"What's the price on the bracelet?" the police officer asked.

"One-hundred-forty-nine dollars," the woman said. "You are fortunate," she told Kit. "This theft is a misdemeanor, which means we can release you to your parents. More than $250 and it would be a felony."

She waited, as if expecting Kit to react but Kit didn't know what to say.

"For a felony," the woman continued, "you'd have to go to the Youth Security Center tonight. Not a pleasant place."

"Not pleasant," echoed the officer. "That's an understatement. But we have to take you people somewhere."

Kit didn't like the way he said, *you people,* as if she were a criminal. Then she realized that, in his view, that's exactly what she was. She had broken the law; that made her a criminal. She wanted to convince him that she wasn't as bad as he thought she was.

"I never took anything before," Kit said.

"That's what they all say," Sergeant Adams said.

"But it's true," Kit said. She could tell he didn't believe her. What good did it do to tell the truth if they weren't going to believe her? Why did he have to treat her like scum, anyway?

A little voice inside Kit's head answered her own question.

31

"Act like a criminal and that's how you'll be treated. You wouldn't have to listen to this if you had not taken the bracelet. You wouldn't be in this office at all."

She said nothing more. She just stared at the floor and waited for Dorothy to arrive. It seemed like hours.

Wayne didn't come with Dorothy. Thank goodness for that, at least. It was bad enough as it was.

"I'm sure Kit didn't mean to steal it," Dorothy said, when she saw the bracelet. "Isn't that right, Kit? You didn't mean to steal it?"

"She meant to steal it, Mrs. Gillette," Sergeant Adams said. "She just didn't mean to get caught."

"Kit has already admitted that she took the bracelet," Mrs. Rydecker said.

Dorothy turned to Kit. "Why?" she said. "Why would you take that? You know better. You know it's wrong to steal."

Kit said nothing. What could she say? That she took the bracelet because Marcia got the part of Frankie and Marcia's father bought her a gold choker and Marcia was a jerk? Or that she took it because her father died ten years ago? Even to her own ears, those excuses made no sense. But there wasn't any other explanation.

Dorothy's eyes narrowed as she looked at Kit. "Did you do this to try to get back at Wayne?" she asked. "Because of the glass?"

Kit shook her head.

"What glass?" asked the woman.

"Oh, nothing," Dorothy said. "Just something that happened at home."

"Tell us about it," the woman said.

Dorothy opened her purse, removed a tissue, and blew her nose. The woman and the officer watched her intently. Kit realized her mother was sorry she had mentioned the glass and was stalling, trying to decide what to say.

"It was just a misunderstanding," Dorothy said. "My husband's hand slipped and the glass he was holding fell and broke and he asked Kit to help clean it up. That's all. Just a little mishap."

"Is that all, Kit?" the woman asked. "Is that what happened?"

"Are you doubting my word?" Dorothy said.

"Not at all. I'm only asking Kit to tell me her version of what happened with the glass."

Kit hesitated. Here was her chance to get even for all the times Dorothy had pretended everything was OK when it wasn't. Here was her chance to make her mother admit the truth about Wayne, not just to Kit but to these people with authority. If she told Sergeant Adams and Mrs. Rydecker that Wayne was drunk and that he threw the glass and it smashed into the refrigerator, and when she refused to clean it up he yelled at her and called her an animal, she knew they would ask more questions. They would want to know if this sort of thing had happened before; did he get drunk often? She could tell the truth, the whole truth and nothing but the truth and maybe her mother would face reality instead of pretending that Wayne was the world's perfect person.

She looked at her mother. Dorothy's eyes were red. She had obviously been crying before she arrived at the store and she had cried again when she heard what Kit had done. Her mother looked suddenly old, more like Grandma Hathaway. Even her hair seemed more gray than Kit remembered.

Dorothy watched Kit warily, waiting for her response.

"My version is the same as hers," Kit said. "Wayne accidentally dropped a glass and broke it. It doesn't have anything to do with the bracelet."

"She's never shoplifted before," her mother said.

"Never shoplifted or never been caught?" Sergeant Adams said.

"Never shoplifted," Kit said.

"Then you are lucky we caught you," Mrs. Rydecker said.

"Lucky!"

"Yes, lucky. If you hadn't been caught, you would have been tempted another time. You would have thought it was easy. You would have kept on taking things until you found yourself in serious trouble."

"She's in serious trouble now," Sergeant Adams said.

Sergeant Adams gave Dorothy some papers to sign. "You'll get a notice in the mail," he told Kit, "telling you when and where to appear."

"You mean I still have to go to court?" Kit asked. "Even though I already gave the bracelet back?"

"If your story checks out," Sergeant Adams said, "and we find that you have no previous record, you won't have to go to court. Instead, you'll appear before a Juvenile Court Committee. It's a panel of three or four people, volunteers, who want to help teenagers. They deal with crimes that occur in their own neighborhoods."

"Are you saying she'll be tried by a bunch of amateurs?" Dorothy asked.

"They've each taken a training program with the court."

"Kit has already admitted her guilt," Mrs. Rydecker pointed out, "so a trial isn't necessary."

"Then why does Kit have to appear before some committee?"

"Because she committed a crime," Mrs. Rydecker replied. "People who commit crimes must be punished." She turned to Kit. "You will have to pay Pierre's a sum for civil restitution," she said, "and you'll have to pay your debt to society, for breaking the law. The committee will decide the best way for you to do that. The courts are too overburdened to hear cases which can be handled in a better way."

"The court committee has legal clout," Sergeant Adams warned. "If you're told to appear, you must do it. Otherwise, we'll issue a warrant for your arrest. You'll be brought in again."

At last, they were allowed to leave. Her mother said nothing as they left the office. Kit trailed her silently through the store, down the escalator, across the mall, and out into the parking lot.

It wasn't until they were both in the car that Dorothy exploded.

"How could you?" she said. "How could you bring such shame on us? We've had our disagreements but I've always been proud of you, always been proud to call you my daughter. Well, I'll tell you something, Kit. Tonight I am not proud."

All day long, Kit had fought back her tears. She had not

cried when she read the cast list, or when Wayne called her an animal. She had not cried when she watched Marcia and Mr. Homer together, or when the police officer announced that she was under arrest. But as she listened to her mother, Kit turned her head away and stared blindly out the window, letting the tears fall unchecked.

CHAPTER
5

NOTHING had changed, yet everything was different.

As Kit walked into Kennedy School the next morning, she felt ten years older than she had the day before.

One day earlier, she could think only of *The Member of the Wedding* and her hopes for the part of Frankie. Now the school play hardly mattered.

She dreaded the court committee meeting. At least in Juvenile Court there was just one judge at a time. This committee business sounded threatening. Three or four adults, instead of one, and all of them against her.

What would her punishment be? She supposed she would have to pay a fine, but how much? Where would she get the money? The thought of asking Wayne to pay it made her sick but she really had no other choice. Briefly, she thought of writing to Grandma and Grandpa Hathaway. When she found out how much the fine was, she could ask them to loan her the money; she could do extra baby-sitting to pay it back. But she knew they wouldn't agree to a loan unless she told them why she needed the money and she would die before she'd let Grandpa and Grandma find out what she had done.

When she left the house that morning, Wayne was still asleep. She didn't know if he knew yet what had happened. Probably not. He had been asleep when Kit and Dorothy got home from Pierre's. Wayne's binges usually lasted three or four days and during that time, there was no use telling him anything. He wouldn't understand it at the time or remember it later. She would have to wait a few days to deal with Wayne's wrath.

"Are you alright?" Tracy asked, as they ate lunch together in the school cafeteria. "You seem sort of distracted."

"I'm OK," Kit said.

"Did you do the Triple-B last night?"

"I couldn't. Wayne the Pain is drinking again and you know how he gets. I didn't stay home."

Tracy nodded sympathetically. "Where did you go?"

"To the mall."

"Alone?"

"I took the bus down and Mom picked me up."

"Did you get anything?"

Yes, Kit thought, I got arrested. She felt her face flush. For a second, she was tempted to tell Tracy the whole story. Maybe it would be easier to deal with if she could talk about it.

She opened her mouth to tell Tracy, but nothing came out.

She couldn't do it. It was too awful. She didn't want Tracy, or anyone else, to know.

She realized Tracy had said something else. "What did you say?"

"What's the matter with you? What happened last night?"

"Nothing."

"I know you better than that." Tracy cocked her head to one side and gave Kit an accusing look. "Did you go out with a guy last night?" she asked.

"No! What makes you think that?"

"You're being so secretive; I thought maybe you had a big date." She switched to the voice she always used when she was Harriet Headline, raunchy reporter. "NINTH-GRADE GIRL ADMITS SECRET LOVE AFFAIR WITH MOVIE STAR."

"If I had a big date, you'd be the first to know." Kit finished her apple and opened her bag of celery sticks. She looked longingly at Tracy's chocolate chip cookies. Dorothy believed only nutritious food belonged in a lunch bag.

"What did happen, then?" Tracy waited. When Kit still said nothing, Tracy said, "OK. You don't have to tell me every detail of your life."

Kit could tell by the way she said it that what Tracy really meant was, you don't have to tell me every detail of your life but I don't understand why you're holding back.

She put the celery sticks back in her lunch bag, crumpled the bag, and tossed it in the trash container. "We get our grades today, for the medical speeches," she said. "I wonder if anyone will get an *A*."

"I doubt it," Tracy said.

On the first day of school, Miss Fenton had announced that she rarely gave an *A* grade. "Anyone who's taking this class to bring their grade-point average up had better transfer out," she said. "I give an *A* only when a speech is truly exceptional. It must make the audience want to applaud, or move them to tears, or give them information which motivates them to take action. In my fourteen years as a speech teacher, I've only given *A* grades twice."

Everyone in the class had groaned at that but it was a challenge. Students in Miss Fenton's class worked hard.

"If anyone deserves an *A* for the medical speech, it is you," Kit said. "Yours was the best speech anyone has done all year."

Tracy beamed.

The assignment had been to talk about any medical topic. Most of the kids picked a disease. Kit gave her speech on hiccups. She did a lot of research and ended with six ways to cure hiccups. The other kids were more interested in her information than in some of the weird diseases people told about. Still, Kit knew her speech was not as good as Tracy's.

Tracy spoke about Alzheimer's disease. Her grandfather had Alzheimer's disease, so Tracy not only gave the medical facts, she explained how the family of a patient feels. When Tracy told the class that her grandfather was in a nursing home and could no longer feed himself, there were tears in her eyes.

She had to pause a moment, to get control of herself. No one moved or spoke. The whole class just sat there in silence until Tracy could continue.

After a moment, Tracy forced a smile and said brightly, "We're pleased with the nursing home. They have lots of special activities, like music and art. A group of Cub Scouts comes sometimes to do a puppet show. Grandpa likes the puppets."

As expected, Miss Fenton handed out grades that day. Before Kit looked at hers, she whispered to Tracy, in her Sharon Shocker accent, "SYNDICATES CLAMOR FOR RIGHT TO PUBLISH SPEECH ON ALZHEIMER'S DISEASE. TV SPECIAL SOLD." Tracy giggled and crossed her fingers.

Kit's grade for the hiccup speech was a *B*. All of her speeches were *B*s. That was better than most of the class got but she wished she could get an *A,* just once. An *A* speech would increase her chances for the scholarship, even without playing the part of Frankie.

Kit watched while Tracy looked at her grade. Tracy shook her head, no, and handed Kit the note from Miss Fenton. Tracy's grade was a *B+*.

"You came close to getting one of my rare *A*s," Miss Fenton had written. "At the end of your speech, when you told about your grandfather in the nursing home, you had a chance to bring your audience to tears by honestly sharing your own emotions. Instead, you chose to dismiss your true feelings and pretend that you were happy."

As usual, Kit thought, Miss Fenton was right. She always was, except for giving the role of Frankie to Marcia. Miss Fenton was wrong that time.

Miss Fenton asked Kit to stay after class that day. When they were alone, Miss Fenton said, "I know you hoped to get the part of Frankie. I want you to know that I think you could handle the part. You might even be a better Frankie than Marcia will be; there's no way for me to be sure. It was a judgment call on my part, that's all. I couldn't cast both of you and when I had to choose, I chose Marcia. That doesn't mean Marcia is a better actress than you are. It only means that this time, I picked her."

Miss Fenton eased herself into her chair. She was a pretty woman, despite her excess weight, and she always dressed with flair. Kit waited.

"When you don't get cast in a show," Miss Fenton continued, "it isn't a rejection of YOU. It only means that this time, with this director, you weren't chosen for a particular part. Another play and another role, the result could be reversed." She smiled at Kit. "You're bright and talented. Next time Marcia can make posters and you can play the lead."

The words were raindrops on Kit's parched pride. She hadn't read poorly, after all. She was just as good an actress as Marcia, maybe even better. And she would have her turn to shine.

She wanted to grab Miss Fenton and whirl her around the room.

Later, she repeated the compliment to herself, considering its implications. Kit knew Miss Fenton was on the selection board for the Ninth Grade Scholarship. If Miss Fenton thought she was bright and talented, maybe she was being considered for the scholarship. Maybe the board members wouldn't find out about the bracelet. Maybe she still had a chance.

Thank goodness she had not told Tracy about the shoplifting. Even though she trusted Tracy not to tell, it was best to keep the matter secret, not take any chance of other people finding out. If Miss Fenton thought she was bright and talented, Kit didn't want to change her opinion.

She decided to start the posters right away, give herself plenty of time and make them extra special. Besides, she needed to do something to take her mind off her problems. If she was thinking about the play, she couldn't worry about what Wayne would say when he found out about the shoplifting, and about her meeting with the court committee.

She hoped she wouldn't have to wait too long to appear before the committee. She wanted to get it over with. The sooner she knew how much the fine was going to be, the sooner she could deal with Wayne's fury.

Three days later, Wayne's car was gone when Kit got home from school. Dorothy was humming in the kitchen, making lasagna. A hot loaf of French bread painted fragrant steam pictures on the windowpane.

"Did Wayne go to work today?" Kit asked.

Dorothy nodded.

"When will he be home?"

"Probably not until seven or so. He had a lot of work to catch up on."

Seven or so. Kit had three hours to figure out what she was going to say to Wayne when he jumped on her about the bracelet. He would do it while they ate dinner. That's when he always discussed any family problems.

She decided that her best defense would be honesty. She would admit it was a terrible thing to do, say she was sorry, and offer to work off the fine in whatever way Wayne wanted.

What if Wayne added his own punishment to whatever the court committee decided? She expected to have to pay Wayne back for any fine she was given; that was only fair. But Wayne would probably decide that wasn't enough. He was a great one for taking away privileges, such as playing the stereo or watching her favorite TV shows. Once he had forbidden her to talk on the telephone for a whole week, just because he'd tried to call home and the line was busy for an hour.

At dinner that night, Kit kept expecting Wayne to mention the shoplifting. Instead, he told Dorothy about something that had happened at work. He went on and on, while Dorothy smiled and nodded.

Kit picked at her food, even though lasagna was one of her favorite dinners and Dorothy hardly ever made it because it was "too fattening." When was he going to yell at her? Was he dragging it out like this on purpose?

She waited.

Wayne took a sip of coffee and turned to Kit. Here it comes, she thought.

"So, Kit," Wayne said. "What's happened at school this week?"

"Not much. Tracy got a part in the play."

"What about you? Didn't you try out for that play?"

"I'm making the posters."

Wayne nodded. "You'll be good at that," he said.

Why was he trying to be nice? This was how he always acted after one of his binges: extra polite, interested in what Kit was doing. She had come to expect this at other times, but not this time. Not after what she'd done.

Finally Kit couldn't stand it any longer. She decided to bring it up herself. Get it over with so she could quit waiting for the storm to break.

44

"About my—uh—problem," she said. "I want you to know . . ."

"Are you sure you don't want some garlic bread?" Dorothy said. "It's especially good tonight."

Surprised, Kit looked at her mother. Dorothy rarely urged Kit to eat anything except vegetables. Usually, she lectured on the hazards of overeating.

"What problem?" Wayne said.

Kit hesitated. Was he being mean, making her spell it out? Or was it possible that Wayne didn't know? "I'm too full for garlic bread," she said.

"What problem?" Wayne said.

"It was nothing, really," Dorothy said. "Kit had some trouble with her math homework while you were sick, that's all, but we figured it out."

"Oh," Wayne said, "a math problem."

"Yes," Dorothy said. "A math problem. Did you ever get it right, Kit?"

"Yes."

"Good. Then we won't have to bother Wayne with it." She looked at Kit.

Kit knew that her mother was telling her that Wayne didn't know about the shoplifting. He didn't know and Dorothy wasn't going to tell him.

"Maybe I have room for garlic bread, after all," Kit said. She took a piece and then took more lasagna, too. Five minutes ago, she had no appetite; now she felt starved.

Later, as she helped Dorothy with the dishes, she whispered, "I was really scared of what Wayne would say."

"I know you've learned a hard lesson from this," Dorothy said, "and I can't see any point in getting your dad all charged up over it."

"What if I have to pay a big fine?"

"I have some money set aside from my household funds. We'll manage, and he won't ever know."

For years, whenever Dorothy covered up Wayne's drinking, Kit had thought it was wrong. It bothered her to hear Dorothy call Wayne's boss and say Wayne was sick and couldn't come to work when in reality Wayne was too drunk to get up off the sofa. It seemed so dishonest to pretend he was sick rather than admit he had a drinking problem.

Now Dorothy was doing the same thing for Kit. She was pretending the shoplifting hadn't happened, telling Wayne that Kit's problem was merely her math homework.

Kit dried the glass salad bowl and put it in the cupboard. Although she was glad Wayne didn't know the truth, she didn't like having Dorothy lie for her. In a way, this was worse than facing Wayne's anger and dealing with it. It made Kit feel scummy. She had done something so low that her own mother couldn't admit it.

Kit wanted to put the whole thing behind her and never think about it again. Dorothy was right about one thing; she had learned a lesson the hard way.

The letter arrived two weeks later. It instructed her to appear before a court committee on April 22, at 7:30 P.M. Her parents were asked to come, too, if possible.

"I'll go with you," Dorothy said.

Kit had mixed feelings about that. On the one hand, she wanted her mother there for moral support. The thought of going alone was too terrifying. On the other hand, she was ashamed to be going at all and it made her shame worse to have her mother witness it.

At least nobody else knew. Not Wayne, not Tracy, not Grandma and Grandpa. And they weren't going to find out, either.

CHAPTER

6

THE phone rang during break-
fast. "Meet me as early as you can," Tracy said. "I have a
surprise." She sounded breathless.

When Kit got to school, she found Tracy pacing the floor
in front of their lockers.

Tracy waved and ran to meet Kit. She thrust an envelope
into Kit's hand. "I mailed the others yesterday," she said. "I
couldn't wait for you to get yours in the mail. Besides, I wanted
to be sure you were the first to know."

Kit had never seen Tracy so excited. She tore open the envelope and withdrew a shiny photograph of a hot air balloon.

"Turn it over," Tracy said. "Read what's on the back."

Kit saw that it was an invitation. She began to read out
loud. "You are invited to a Hot Air Balloon Birthday Party.

Where: Meet in the school parking lot; you'll be driven to the launch site. When . . ."

Before she could finish, Tracy broke in. "Isn't it super? My parents have reserved three hot air balloons. We take off from that old airport south of town, the one that isn't used for planes anymore. There are 'chase vans' that follow the balloons, on the ground. When we land, the vans will be there to take us home. But first we'll have sparkling cider and a picnic dinner. All the food will be in the vans, even a birthday cake."

Tracy paused to catch her breath.

"That," Kit said, "is the most fantastic party I ever heard of." Tracy's parents always had original ideas. Usually Tracy's birthday parties weren't this lavish but they were always different and always fun. How wonderful it would be to have parents like that.

"I've thought of some great headlines. Listen to this: 'PARTY GIRLS GET HIGH IN BALLOONS'."

Kit giggled.

"Or how about, 'BASKET CASE DISAPPEARS IN CLOUDS.' Get it? We ride in the balloon's basket."

Kit groaned but she couldn't resist slipping into Sharon Shocker's voice and saying, "BALLOON PARTY INVITATIONS HOT ITEM ON BLACK MARKET. SCALPERS GET THOUSANDS." She looked again at her invitation. "Who else did you invite?" she asked.

"All the girls who are in the play." Tracy started naming her guests but Kit didn't hear the names.

Kit stopped walking. She had just read the rest of the invitation. *"When: April 22 at 5 P.M."*

On April 22 at 7:30 she had to appear before the Juvenile

49

Court Committee. "What time will the party end?" she asked.

"The balloons will land around seven. It'll take an hour for the picnic and then my parents will drive everybody home. It won't be late; probably nine o'clock."

Nine o'clock. She licked her lips and swallowed. She felt as if she'd just been punched in the stomach. She had to miss Tracy's party.

"What's the matter?" Tracy said. "Don't you think I should have invited Marcia? I didn't really want to but I didn't see how I could leave her out when I'm asking the rest of the girls in the cast. Besides, she's doing a good job in the play. You should come to a rehearsal; you'd be amazed how hard she works. And she hardly brags at all."

"I can't go."

"Why not? Miss Fenton doesn't care, as long as you're quiet."

Kit shook her head, pointing to the invitation. "I can't go," she repeated.

"You can't go on the balloon ride?" Tracy's voice rose on the last word, ending in a little squeak.

Kit nodded her head. "That's right. I can't go to your party."

"Why not?"

"I—I just can't."

"But you have to come! This is the kind of birthday I've always dreamed of and you're my best friend. It won't be any fun if you aren't there."

"I'm sorry," Kit said. "I want to come, believe me." She looked again at the invitation. "Your birthday is April twenty-third," she said. "Why is the party on the twenty-second?"

"Dad couldn't get all three balloons on the twenty-third." The excitement was gone from Tracy's voice. She looked at Kit with narrowed eyes, as if by squinting she would be able to see inside Kit's head and discover what she was thinking. "Kit, you *have* to come. Can't you change whatever plans you have for that day?"

Kit shook her head. No, she thought. I cannot tell the court committee, sorry, I can't make it, I'm going to a birthday party. "I wish I could."

"Then at least tell me what you're doing that day. If it's so important, I think . . ."

"I can't tell you." Kit didn't mean to sound cross but that's the way it came out.

"Well, excuse me," Tracy said.

Kit knew Tracy was hurt and she didn't blame her. It was bad enough not to go to the party; it was even worse not to explain why.

"I'd tell you if I could," Kit said. "But I can't. You're just going to have to trust me."

Tracy spoke softly. "If anybody else I invited can't come, it won't make that much difference. You're the only one who really matters. Maybe I should have checked the date with you before we sent out the invitations but I thought it would be fun to surprise you and I never thought you'd have to be somewhere else. You never mentioned anything and . . ." She stopped suddenly and gave Kit the squint-eyed look again. "You aren't in some kind of trouble, are you?" she asked.

"No," Kit said quickly. "What makes you think that?"

"If you are," Tracy said, "you can tell me."

"I'm not in any trouble."

"Good." From the way Tracy said, "Good," Kit could tell she was not totally convinced.

Kit looked again at the picture of the balloon. It was a round multicolored checkerboard, with squares of yellow, orange, red, green, and lavender, against a blue sky. A square wicker basket hung below it, carrying people high above the trees. She couldn't see their faces but she was sure they were smiling.

"You'll have a great time, whether I'm there or not," she said. "It's a wonderful party idea."

"It won't be the same without you."

By the next day, other people had received their invitations. Linda, who was in Kit's and Tracy's speech class, swooped in, waving her invitation like a signal flag.

"I'll be there," she told Tracy. "Wild horses couldn't keep me away. Ever since I saw the movie *Around the World in Eighty Days,* I've ached to go up in a hot air balloon." She turned to Kit. "What are you going to wear that night?" she asked.

Kit licked her lips, wondering what to say. "I—don't know," she said. If she told Linda that she wasn't going on the balloon ride, Linda would want to know why. Kit could see that her secret would quickly become an even bigger problem than it already was if people knew she wasn't going to Tracy's balloon party. Linda assumed that Kit would be there. Everyone else would assume the same thing. And why not? She and Tracy were best friends. She had never missed one of Tracy's birthday parties before.

"Wear something cool," Tracy said. "We were told it gets warm in the balloon from the gas jets. Bring a jacket, though, because by the time the picnic is over, it will probably be dark, and chilly."

"What if it rains?" Linda asked. "Will we still go?"

"If it rains, or if it's too windy, we have to postpone the balloon ride. We'll still have the picnic, but it would be indoors, at my house."

Linda pressed the palms of her hands together, looked up, and closed her eyes. "Let us pray for sunshine," she said.

"I already am," Tracy said.

As Linda babbled about the balloon ride, Kit gave Tracy a grateful look. Tracy could have told Linda that Kit wasn't going to the party. When she didn't, Kit knew she wouldn't tell anyone else, either. They wouldn't know that Kit wasn't coming until they were ready to launch the balloons. By then, everyone would be so excited, they might not even miss her. If they did, if anyone asked her the next day why she wasn't there, she would say she got sick.

Another lie, Kit thought. I'll create a new secret to cover up the old one. She didn't like to pretend she was going when she knew that she wasn't, but she couldn't think what else to do.

As Linda and Tracy discussed how it might feel to go up in a balloon, Kit wondered if she should tell Tracy the truth. Maybe she owed Tracy that much. Tracy was loyal. That's why Tracy hadn't told Linda. Tracy realized how awkward it would be for Kit if everyone knew she wasn't going to the party but wouldn't say why. Gossip would fly faster than a spaceship.

She could just imagine the speculation: Tracy and Kit had a terrible fight and Tracy didn't invite Kit to her party. Or, Kit's been grounded for a month and her parents aren't letting her go to Tracy's party. Then everyone would try to guess WHY Kit was grounded. Failing grades? Stayed out all night? Smoking? It would go on and on. She knew it and Tracy knew it, too. That's why Tracy didn't tell Linda.

Tracy deserves to know why I can't go, Kit thought. But if I tell her the truth—tell her that I stole a bracelet and have to appear before a court committee—will she still feel the same toward me? Will she still be loyal or will she be so shocked that she backs off from me?

Once, when they were eight years old, Kit and Tracy had formed a secret club. They called it the TRIK CLUB, using the first two initials of their names, and their motto was: Be brave, be honest, be good. I messed up on all three counts, Kit thought.

Tracy was the only person in the world who had always believed in Kit. Tracy always took Kit's side. She still thought Kit was brave, honest, and good. How could Kit risk losing that?

She said nothing.

Secretly, she hoped it would rain on April 22. The balloon ride would get rescheduled and she would go and no one would be the wiser. Then she felt guilty for wanting rain to spoil Tracy's party.

The scene with Linda repeated itself with variations during the next two weeks because everyone who was going on the balloon ride thought Kit was going, too. It soon required no effort to pretend that she was.

The more I lie, Kit thought, the easier it gets.

Tracy had play rehearsal after school every day so they had less time together than usual. Kit thought it was just as well. She would be glad when April 22nd was over, for more reasons than one.

The day finally arrived: sunny, clear, and still. A perfect day for a hot air balloon trip.

After school, Tracy made a point of getting Kit alone for a moment. "If your plans change, even at the last minute," she said, "you can still come. I didn't invite anyone else to take your place, so there's an extra space in one balloon."

"I won't be there," Kit said.

Tracy said nothing.

"I hope you have a great time tonight," Kit said.

"Thanks. You, too."

Not much chance of that, Kit thought. She was far more nervous about going before the court committee than she had ever been about anything in her life. The night before, she had dreamed about it—a weird, scary dream where a whole group of people pointed at her, shouting, "Guilty! Guilty! Guilty!"

When Kit got home from school, Dorothy had on her good suit. "You should wear a dress, too," she told Kit. "First impressions are important."

Kit agreed.

"I told your dad that we're going to a meeting at school tonight. If he says anything to you, you'd better have the same story."

"All right." It was a good excuse; Wayne never attended any of the school functions, even those where the parents were specifically invited. Still, Kit hated making up another story. All she'd done for the last two weeks was pretend. Her whole life was becoming one big lie.

Well, she thought, it will soon be over. I've kept my secret and once I've faced the committee and paid my fine or whatever they tell me to do, that will be the end of it. No one I know will ever find out what happened.

They had an early dinner but Kit had no appetite.

Neither of them spoke during the drive to City Hall. They parked and walked past a bed of purple crocuses and yellow daffodils, up the steps to City Hall. Two flags flew at the top of a tall metal pole, causing a chain to clink rhythmically. It seemed to match the pounding of Kit's heart.

What would the committee do? Lecture her? Assess a big fine? Would she be put on probation and have to report weekly to a probation officer?

They were early. Dorothy perched on one of the benches in the lobby but Kit was too nervous to sit. She looked at the framed pictures of the Mayor and the City Council members. She stood before the bulletin board and read all the notices: public hearings, where to donate blood, the Lion's Club pancake breakfast. She saw a rack of bus schedules and a table with forms to fill out, to report an automobile accident.

Dorothy took the letter from her purse and looked at it. "Upstairs," she said. "We're supposed to go to the second floor."

They climbed the stairs. A door at the top had a sign on it: Juvenile Court Diversion Committee.

"What time is it?" Kit asked.

"Seven twenty."

Ten more minutes. Kit felt perspiration under her arms. She hoped she wouldn't ruin her good dress.

There was a candy machine in the hall, plus a table and a few chairs. They sat down.

Kit heard loud voices and a clatter of footsteps. Two boys, both about seventeen, ran up the stairs.

"This is it," the tall one said, as he pointed to the door. "The committee for rowdy delinquents." Both boys laughed loudly.

They went to the candy machine, inserted quarters, and bought candy bars. The tall boy threw his candy wrapper on the floor.

"You coming in with me?" the short one asked.

"They won't let me. But there's nothing to it. They'll ask you to be a good little boy and you promise that you will and that's it. When my brother got arrested, they . . ."

"Keith got arrested? What did he get arrested for?"

"Murder."

"Murder?" The short boy looked dubious. "No way."

The tall boy laughed. "No kidding," he said. "He was driving Dad's boat and he ran over a girl who was swimming in the lake. Never saw her. Didn't even know he hit her. That night, the cops came to our house. Somebody had reported the boat and Keith was accused of murder."

Both boys guffawed again. Kit knew they were acting smart partly because of her. She ignored them.

"Only my brother could murder someone and not even know he did it!" The boys hooted louder.

Beside her, Kit felt Dorothy cringe in disgust.

Kit remembered Sergeant Adams saying, "We have to take you people somewhere." If these two creeps were typical of the kids Sergeant Adams dealt with, Kit could understand why he hadn't believed her that night.

She wondered why the short boy had to appear before the committee. What had he done? His smartmouth friend obviously had been here before but the short one, despite his bravado, seemed apprehensive. He kept rubbing his fingers together and he didn't finish his candy bar. Kit wondered where his parents were. Why did he have to bring his show-off friend with him, instead of his dad or mom?

Kit knew how hard it was for Dorothy, who always denied that any problem existed, to admit that Kit had shoplifted. Yet Dorothy was there, by Kit's side. "Thanks for coming with me," she whispered.

Just then the door opened. A man in dark coveralls and a girl in jeans came out. As they went down the stairs, Kit heard the man say, "I didn't need this, you know. My boss asked me to stay late tonight. My first chance this month for overtime pay and I have to turn it down so I can go with my daughter, the thief, and get insulted by a bunch of . . ."

A woman came out of the room. "Kit Hathaway?" she said. Kit stood.

She and Dorothy entered the committee room. It was not a formal arrangement, like a courtroom. Instead, there were chairs in a circle, with two empty chairs for Kit and Dorothy.

Kit started to follow Dorothy to their places. Then she saw the members of the committee.

She stopped. In her worst fears of what would happen at this meeting, she never imagined anything this bad. Even her dream, with the crowd shouting, "Guilty!" was better than this.

There, in the chair nearest the door, sat Miss Fenton.

CHAPTER
7

KIT wanted to run.

Miss Fenton was on the committee. Kit's favorite teacher would hear the whole story of how Kit tried to steal a bracelet in Pierre's. How bright and talented would she think Kit was now?

She couldn't run. Sergeant Adams had said if she didn't appear as scheduled, she would be arrested again. All she could do was go in and sit down. She would live through this. Somehow.

She sat beside her mother, carefully avoiding Miss Fenton's eyes.

The other people introduced themselves as Mr. Cramer and Mrs. Phillips.

Mrs. Phillips was the spokesperson for the group. First she read a long statement that explained how the committee works.

It said Kit could have a lawyer if she wanted one and if she chose not to participate in this meeting, her case would go to court.

Kit and Dorothy signed the paper, agreeing that they understood it.

"Kit?" It was Miss Fenton. "Do you want me to excuse myself from your case? This hearing is confidential, of course. No committee member will discuss a case outside of this room, but since we know each other, you may ask to have someone else sit in my place. We can set a new time for you to appear."

"You know each other?" Dorothy said.

"Miss Fenton is my speech teacher," Kit said. She felt miserable. She didn't want Miss Fenton on the committee because she didn't want Miss Fenton to know about this. But since Miss Fenton obviously did know, there wasn't much point in asking her to be replaced and postponing the whole mess any longer.

"Let's just go ahead," Kit said.

"We want you to understand that this is not a trial," Mrs. Phillips said. "The question of guilt or innocence has already been settled. What we are concerned about here is why this happened and what we can do to keep it from happening again. We will be speaking with each of you privately. You first, Mrs. Gillette. Kit, you may wait outside."

Kit went back to the waiting area. Relieved that the rowdy boys were gone, she sank into a chair. I'll never get to college, she thought. Miss Fenton wouldn't tell anyone what Kit had done but she wouldn't want Kit to win the scholarship now, either. Of all the people who might be on a court committee, why did it have to be her?

Ten minutes later, Dorothy came out and said, "They want to talk to you now and I'm supposed to wait out here."

Kit returned to the committee.

Miss Fenton spoke first. "Whatever you tell us here will not be repeated to anyone," she said. "Not to your mother, not to anyone else."

"According to the police report," Mr. Cramer said, "you were not on drugs and you have no previous record. You have never been in trouble at school, either. Is that right, Kit?"

"Yes."

"Why did you take the bracelet?"

"I don't know," Kit said. "It was stupid."

"Suppose you tell us what else happened that day, before you got to Pierre's."

"Everything went wrong. I decided to go to the mall and when I got there, I saw a girl I know from school. She's always bragging and acting like a queen and she was there with her father and he was buying her anything she wanted. She asked me to help her choose which piece of jewelry she should get."

"Go on," Mrs. Phillips said.

"I looked at the trays of jewelry and I thought the one bracelet was really pretty."

"And that's why you took it? Because you liked it?"

"Yes. I mean, no. I mean, it isn't quite that simple. It was partly because I liked it but mostly it was because Marcia was the one who got the part I wanted in the school play, and then her father was there, smiling and buying her an expensive present and it made me lonesome for my own dad."

"Do you usually go to the mall alone?"

"No."

61

"Why did you go that night?"

"I just wanted to."

"Was there a problem at home?"

Kit thought about Wayne. Should she tell these people about Wayne's binges? What would it accomplish, except to make her mother miserable.

"No," Kit said. "There was no problem at home."

"You said earlier that everything had gone wrong that day. Can you be more specific? Exactly what went wrong?"

Kit looked at Miss Fenton. She wished now that she had asked Miss Fenton to be replaced by someone she didn't know. "I guess it started at school. I tried out for the spring play and I thought I had a good chance of getting the lead role. Instead, I didn't get a part at all."

"What else went wrong?" Mr. Cramer said.

"That's all."

"According to our report, your mother asked you if you were trying to get back at your stepfather because of something to do with a glass," Mr. Cramer said. "Tell us what happened with the glass."

Kit looked at the three adults. She knew she could easily win their sympathy if she told them that Wayne went on drunken binges and that he had thrown a glass against the refrigerator and ordered her to clean up the mess. If she also told them how he yelled at her, they'd really feel sorry for her.

But she couldn't do it. Don't hang your dirty laundry in public. That's what Grandma Hathaway always said. Kit knew these people were trying to help her, but she decided to protect Dorothy from prying eyes. Dorothy was here tonight; Kit had not had to come alone. Since Dorothy had kept Kit's secret, the least Kit could do was return the favor.

"There isn't anything to tell," she said. "Wayne accidentally broke a glass, that's all."

"That's the whole story?" Mrs. Phillips said.

"Yes."

The three committee members exchanged glances.

"All right," Mrs. Phillips said. "Let's proceed."

"When the court committee is convinced that someone will not commit another crime," Miss Fenton said, "we sometimes offer that person a contract."

"What kind of contract?"

"A contract to work off your debt to society. For example, if we believe that you will not shoplift again, we might let you make amends in a way that will allow you to have your criminal record erased."

"How?" Kit said. "What would I have to do?"

"You would agree to do community service for a nonprofit organization," Mrs. Phillips said. "If you fulfill the agreement and if you have no other charges filed against you for two years, the charges of shoplifting would be dropped."

"Dropped?"

"It would be dismissed entirely," Mr. Cramer said. "The court would destroy all record of this offense."

"It would be as if you had never been caught shoplifting," Mrs. Phillips said.

It was almost too good to be true. All she had to do was work for some group and her record would be clean.

"May I do that?"

"Is that what you want?"

"Yes."

"You may wait in the hall with your mother now," Miss Fenton said. "We'll call you both back in as soon as we decide how to proceed with your case."

Kit and Dorothy waited silently for the committee's decision. From inside the room came the rapid clacking of a typewriter. Kit crossed her fingers.

In a few minutes, Miss Fenton came to the door and asked them to come back in.

Mrs. Phillips shuffled some papers on her desk. "We are prepared to offer you a contract, Kit," she said. "You will do twenty hours of volunteer work for The Humane Society. Your work must be verified by a staff member. When you've completed that amount of time, the staff member will notify us. Two years from now, if you stay out of trouble, this charge will be dropped. Do you want to accept the contract?"

"Yes."

"We want both of you to read it carefully before you sign," Mrs. Phillips said, as she handed Kit and Dorothy each a copy. "Notice that there are time limits for completing your community service work."

Kit read the contract carefully. Mrs. Phillips signed it for the committee, and Dorothy signed where it said, "Parent or Guardian."

As Kit wrote her name, she felt light as a soap bubble. If she weren't indoors, she might drift upwards and float across the treetops, like Mary Poppins. She didn't have to be on probation. She didn't have to pay a fine. Best of all, no record of what she had done would remain to haunt her in the future.

No one except the people in this room would ever know and they had each promised not to tell. Her secret was safe forever. At that moment, she didn't even care that she was missing Tracy's party.

As they left City Hall, Dorothy said, "Is that the speech teacher you're always talking about? The one who's so terrific?"

"Yes."

"She must weigh two hundred pounds. What's so terrific about that?"

"She does interesting things. She plays the harp for wedding receptions and she leads tours of the zoo."

Dorothy sniffed. "She'd fit right in, with the hippos."

Kit decided to change the subject. She knew there was no way her mother would ever see what a vibrant, exciting person Miss Fenton was. Dorothy couldn't see past the excess pounds on Miss Fenton's hips.

"I don't know anything about The Humane Society," she said. "Do you?"

"All I know," said Dorothy, "is that they take care of unwanted animals."

"I wonder what they'll have me do."

"Clean out the cages, I expect."

A tiny pinprick pierced Kit's soap bubble. Oh, great. For twenty hours, she would serve the community by shoveling dog piles.

The next morning, she took Tracy's birthday gift to school. It was a small picture frame, molded of clay, with bears on it. Tracy collected teddy bears and Kit was sure she would love the picture frame.

Tracy hardly had time to look at it because a group of kids crowded around, asking about the balloon ride.

"It was fantastic!" Tracy said. "We saw our balloons reflected in the water when we went over a river. And we startled some deer and watched them run into the woods."

"We could look down on the tops of the trees," Linda said, "and when we drifted over a farmhouse, the children ran out and waved and called. They looked like little dolls down below."

People followed Tracy around all day, asking questions. You'd think Tracy was a national hero, or something. You'd think she and Linda were the first people to walk on Mars.

Even when Kit was alone with her, Tracy didn't want to talk about anything else. She never did thank Kit for the picture frame. Not that Kit cared about being thanked. She just didn't like being left out. She felt as if everyone who had gone on the balloon ride belonged to an exclusive club and she could never be a member.

It wasn't until classes were over that Tracy asked Kit about her evening. "Did everything go OK for you last night?" she said.

"Yes."

Tracy cocked her head to one side and gave Kit a piercing look. "Care to tell me about it?"

Kit shook her head.

"So be a mystery woman," Tracy said. "Who cares?" She walked away, leaving Kit alone at their lockers.

It was the first time Kit could ever remember Tracy being angry with her. Not that she blamed Tracy. She *was* acting mysterious; she knew that.

Kit put on her sweater, picked up her bookbag, and slammed her locker shut. She didn't like alienating Tracy. She didn't like it one bit.

She leaned against her locker and closed her eyes. What was she going to do now? Not even the Triple-B would help if she lost Tracy's friendship.

"Kit?" It was Miss Fenton.

Kit straightened and forced a smile.

"Could I speak to you for a moment, in my room?"

Miss Fenton closed the door and gestured for Kit to sit down. "Last night," she said, "I sensed that you were not telling the whole story. I think perhaps you *do* have a problem at home and I want to help you, if you need it. Not as a member of the committee. Because I care about you."

"Thanks."

Miss Fenton waited. Kit looked at her shoes.

"There's no shame in having a problem," Miss Fenton said. "The only shame is in not trying to correct the problem."

Like Dorothy, Kit thought.

"I feel something else happened that night, before you went to the mall. Something to do with your stepfather. Do you want to talk about it?"

Suddenly, Kit did want to talk about it. The whole story spilled out: Wayne's binges, Dorothy covering up for him, Kit's frustration.

When she finished, Miss Fenton asked, "Have you talked to your mother about this?"

"It doesn't do any good. She pretends everything is OK." Kit couldn't keep the bitterness out of her voice. "She only sees what she wants to see."

67

"Don't be too hard on her. It's difficult to be caught in someone else's trap."

Kit sniffed.

"Do you feel able to cope with the situation?"

"Yes."

"You're sure? You have a bright future, Kit. I don't want you to spoil it."

"I can cope."

"If that changes—if you feel threatened or afraid or just pushed too far—will you tell me, or tell someone else who's in a position to help?"

Kit nodded.

Miss Fenton stood up. "I won't repeat this conversation," she said. "Thank you for being honest with me. The shoplifting was so out of character for you and you looked so unhappy there by your locker, I was afraid you had a problem you couldn't handle."

I do, Kit thought, remembering Tracy's anger. But that wasn't something Miss Fenton could help with.

CHAPTER
8

THE noise was loud; it was frantic. The dogs sounded desperate, as if they believed that if they barked loudly enough, someone would surely let them out.

The barking began as soon as she entered the kennel building. Some dogs leaped into the air; some pawed at the doors of their cages, trying to get her attention. Others cowered in a corner, watching her warily. One, in his haste to be noticed, stepped in his bowl of food, spilling kibble across the floor.

Kit put her hands over her ears as she walked slowly down the concrete walkway. There were cages on both sides of her, each containing one or more dogs. The cages were clean; the animals all had water and some had blankets to sleep on. It was clear that they were being cared for as well as possible, given the circumstances. It was equally clear that food, water, and housing were not all they needed.

Their eyes followed Kit and the barking grew more frenzied as she continued.

Her assignment was to "socialize" the dogs.

When she had arrived that afternoon for her first two-hour stint, she met Lynnette, the manager. Lynnette was a friendly young woman who acted pleased to have Kit there.

"What do you know about The Humane Society?" she asked.

Kit admitted she didn't know anything.

"We are not the 'dog pound'," Lynnette said. "We don't pick up stray animals or enforce leash laws. That's done by the county animal control, which is entirely separate from us. We're a nonprofit organization, affiliated with the Society for the Prevention of Cruelty to Animals. We investigate cruelty cases and we try to provide homes for unwanted animals."

She gave Kit a quick tour of the main building. In addition to the large room where the adoption desk was, there was a cat room with floor-to-ceiling cages, a spay/neuter clinic, Lynnette's office, and a volunteer station.

Lynnette wrote *KIT, Volunteer* on a nametag and handed it to Kit. "Today, I'd like you to socialize the dogs," Lynnette said. "You can sit with them in the cages, if you want. Pet them and talk to them. Or you can take them out to the exercise yard, one at a time. It's fenced, so once you're in the yard, you can remove the leash and let the dog run free. There are balls for them to play with and poop-scoops for you to clean the yard with, if you need to."

As she talked, she led Kit out a side door and pointed to

the exercise yard. It was surrounded by an eight-foot-high chain link fence.

"Before we began our volunteer program," Lynnette said, "some dogs became unadoptable and had to be euthanized because they were so withdrawn. They don't understand why they're here; it's natural for them to pull back and be distrustful. Since we began using volunteers to socialize the dogs, we haven't had to euthanize a single animal because it became antisocial." She spoke with pride. Kit could tell that the animals were important to Lynnette.

"Have you ever had a dog, Kit?"

"No, but I've always wanted one."

Lynnette took a yellow leash from a hook and handed it to Kit. Then she led the way to the kennel.

"Be careful when you open a cage door," she said. "The dogs will try to get out." She demonstrated how to do it, using her knee to block the space as she eased the door of the first cage open and slipped inside. Then she came back out and had Kit do it. As soon as she was in the cage, Kit began petting and talking to the black lab inside.

"Don't spend too much time with any one animal," Lynnette said. "I wouldn't want you to get overly attached."

It seemed an odd remark for someone whose business was trying to find homes for unwanted pets.

Lynnette watched while Kit put the leash on the lab and took it to the exercise yard. When Kit had put the lab safely back in his cage, Lynnette returned to the office.

Kit walked slowly through the kennel while the dogs on both sides leaped and yipped.

A sheet of paper was clipped to the front of each cage. It

told how old the dog was, its name, and any known background information. There was a blank space where Kit was supposed to write the date and how much time she spent with each dog.

"Do as many as you can," Lynnette had said. "I know you won't have time to do them all so try to do those who haven't had a volunteer visit recently."

The last cage in the row contained a medium-sized terrier with reddish-blonde fur. Unlike the others, this dog didn't bark and didn't jump around. It just sat on the floor, staring balefully up at Kit. Kit looked at the paper on the cage.

Terrier mix. Approx. 2 years old. Found abandoned in a freeway rest stop.

Someone had added a date and: "Socialized, 10 min. I called her Lady." The date was more than a week ago.

Kit lifted the latch on the cage, carefully slipped inside, and closed the door.

"Hello, Lady," she said.

Lady stood up and her tail wagged tentatively.

Kit sat down. She was surprised to find that the concrete floor was warm. The kennel must have some kind of radiant heat.

"Good dog," she said. "Good Lady."

The terrier sat next to Kit, leaning against her. There was a metal dog door on the back wall which could be opened or closed from the front of the cage. Peering through the open door, she saw that the kennel continued on the outside of the building.

Kit scratched Lady's ears. The rest of Lady's fur was coarse

72

and wiry but her ears were like rust-colored velvet. Lady leaned closer, until she flopped over sideways onto Kit's lap.

Kit laughed and rubbed the dog's stomach. Lady wriggled with pleasure and licked Kit's arm.

"You're a fine dog," Kit said. Did Lady jump out of the car and run off while her family was traveling? Or did someone purposely leave her at the rest stop? She wondered how anyone could have left such a nice dog behind.

Kit slipped the looped end of the leash over Lady's neck, and pulled it snug. Then she stood up and opened the cage door. Instantly, Lady bounded out the door and trotted down the kennel walkway, toward the yard. Kit held tightly to the leash and ran along behind. She opened the gate to the exercise area and took Lady inside. After making sure the gate was securely closed again, she removed the leash.

Lady galloped back and forth. She sniffed the ground; she sniffed the fence. Kit picked up a tennis ball and threw it. Lady ran after it but she wouldn't bring it back to Kit. Instead, she ran in circles around the yard, with the ball in her mouth.

Kit threw a second ball. Lady promptly dropped the first ball and charged after the second one. Then she ran laps with that one in her mouth. Her tail streamed out behind her and her ears flapped up and down as she ran.

It must feel good, Kit thought, to run like that after she's been caged for so long. She threw the balls until Lady's tongue hung sideways out of her mouth. Lady still wanted to play but Kit was afraid to overdo it. She put the leash back on Lady and took her back to the kennel.

As soon as they approached the kennel, Lady hung back.

Kit had to tug on the leash to get Lady to walk beside her, back to her cage. When Kit opened the cage door, Lady braced her feet and leaned away from the cage, refusing to go in.

"You have to go back in," Kit said. "I'm sorry, Lady." She gave the terrier a hard push but Lady didn't budge. Finally Kit had to get back inside the cage herself, and pull Lady in after her. Once Lady was inside, Kit removed the leash and slipped back out. As she latched the door, Lady sat in the corner of the cage and looked up at Kit. Her brown eyes seemed to beg, "Couldn't I go home with you? Couldn't you take me home?"

Kit wrote the date and "Socialized" on Lady's paper. She looked at her watch, surprised to see that thirty minutes had passed already. She wrote, "30 min.," feeling guilty that she'd spent so long with Lady when Lynnette had asked her to do as many dogs as possible. Still, it hadn't seemed like nearly enough time for Lady. Trying not to look at the terrier's sad brown eyes, Kit went on to another cage.

This one contained three black puppies. Kit sat on the floor and let the puppies crawl on her, chew her shoelaces, lick her fingers. She petted them and talked to them but she didn't take them out of their cage. The note on their cage said only, "Six weeks old. Owner can't keep. Too many puppies."

Next she took a big dog, part-German shepherd and part collie, out to the yard and let him run. The dog trotted along next to her on the leash and when she threw the ball, he brought it back and dropped it in front of her. She only kept him in the yard for ten minutes. It didn't seem like much exercise for such a big dog but there were so many others, all waiting a turn.

She socialized ten dogs that day, counting the three puppies. Only ten out of—how many? Kit did a quick count. Fifty. Maybe more. Many of the cages contained more than one dog. She hadn't even tried to do anything with them because she was afraid one would get loose while she tried to remove the other. She wanted to stay longer than two hours, but she had a baby-sitting job at 6:30.

She went back to Lynnette's office. Lynnette looked up as Kit approached. "How did it go?" she asked.

"I only did seven dogs, plus three puppies," Kit said. "I tried to hurry, but . . ."

Lynnette smiled at her. "Each one deserves your full two hours," she said. "If you did ten, you did well." She picked up a folder with Kit's name on it, opened it, and recorded the time inside. "Thank you, Kit," she said. "I'll see you again on Friday."

On Friday, Lynnette said, "You know what to do. Just start where you left off last time."

Kit put on her nametag, took a leash, and entered the kennel. This time, she was prepared for the noise.

She walked quickly to the last cage and looked inside. Lady wagged her tail vigorously.

Kit hesitated. She knew she was supposed to give the others a turn but Lady was so glad to see her.

"We'll hurry," Kit said, as she opened the cage and dropped the leash around Lady's neck. "Just a quick game of ball."

Lady danced around her, clearly overjoyed to see Kit again.

This time, it was harder to put Lady back in the cage. Her

tail drooped and her head hung. She slunk to the back of the cage and lay down with her nose on her paws.

"I'm sorry," Kit whispered. "I'm sorry, but all the others want to get out for awhile, too."

She wrote the date and time on Lady's paper, noting that no one else had socialized Lady since Kit's last visit, three days ago. At the top of each paper was the date when the animal had been brought in. Lady had been there for two weeks. That's a long time to sit in a cage and wait, Kit thought. No wonder some of the dogs gave up hope.

There were only two puppies in the cage where she'd sat last time. Kit smiled, knowing one of the pups must have been adopted. She passed that cage by and went on to those she hadn't done before.

Kit played with twelve dogs that day, everything from a wriggly black-and-white dustmop to a stately Afghan. Before she left, she slipped into Lady's cage for a few minutes and sat on the floor. Instantly, Lady was on Kit's lap, trembling with pleasure.

Kit leaned against the side of the cage and looked out through the wire. It was like being in prison. She stroked Lady's head and talked quietly to her.

"Maybe someone will adopt you soon," Kit said. "A nice family, with children for you to play with. They'll have a yard for you to run in and plenty of doggie toys and a soft bed, all your own."

Lady licked Kit's fingers; her tail thumped on the concrete floor. Kit leaned over and buried her face in Lady's fur. Then she wrinkled up her nose. "The first thing your new family will do," she said, "is give you a bath."

76

Lady's tail thumped some more.

"You silly dog," Kit said. "You don't care what I say, do you, as long as I talk to you?"

Lady's tail wagged harder.

Kit smiled and rubbed Lady's velvety ears. "If I could have a dog," she said, "I'd have one just like you."

For her seventh birthday, Kit had asked for a puppy. Dorothy explained that they couldn't have a dog because no one was home all day and the puppy would be lonely. Kit was disappointed, but she had accepted the decision.

After Dorothy married Wayne and quit her job, Kit asked again. Although Dorothy's excuse that time was that Kit was too young to be responsible for a dog, Kit overheard Wayne say dogs were expensive and she sensed that no matter how responsible she was, the answer would be the same. She had never asked again.

Now Kit stroked Lady's fur thoughtfully. Dorothy no longer had a secretarial job; she was home all day. Certainly Kit was old enough to take full responsibility for a pet. She could even pay for Lady's food, with the money she earned baby-sitting. She already had enough saved to pay The Humane Society's adoption fee.

A tingle of excitement prickled the back of Kit's neck. She couldn't think of a single valid reason for Dorothy and Wayne to say *no*.

She stood. "Good-bye, Lady," she said. "Maybe you'll see me again tomorrow, with good news. Keep your paws crossed."

As she gave Lady one final pat, the incessant barking stopped. Kit listened, surprised to hear music in the kennel. Someone was playing "April Showers" on a harmonica.

Curious, she slipped out of Lady's cage and looked to see where the music was coming from.

A chubby man sat on a folding campstool, just inside the kennel door. With his gray hair, bushy beard, and abundant belly, he looked exactly like Santa Claus, except that he wore bib overalls, a green plaid shirt, and a baseball cap. He also wore a volunteer nametag.

He leaned toward the nearest cage as he played, serenading the dogs. When he saw Kit, his eyes crinkled but he kept playing. She listened until the song ended, watching the dogs.

"They like it," Kit said.

"Music hath charms to soothe the savage beast," he said.

"It hasn't been this quiet in here since I arrived."

"That's why I come, girl. Best audience in town. They love every tune I play and they never request anything I don't know." He put out his hand. "I'm Randall Morrison," he said.

"Kit Hathaway."

They shook hands and then Mr. Morrison put the harmonica to his mouth and began to play, "I've Been Working on the Railroad."

As the peppy music filled the air, Kit could have sworn that some of the dogs were wagging their tails in 4/4 time.

She wondered if Mr. Morrison was a volunteer by choice or if, like she, he was doing community service to atone for some trouble with the law. She couldn't imagine such a jolly-looking person getting arrested.

All the way home on the bus, she rehearsed how she would tell Dorothy and Wayne her plan to adopt Lady. By the time she reached her bus stop, she knew exactly what she wanted to say.

It took willpower not to blurt out her speech the minute she got home, but she knew Wayne was always more agreeable after he ate.

She sniffed. Good. Pot roast. Wayne's favorite meal.

She waited until they were almost finished eating. Then she couldn't stand it any longer. Trying to sound casual, she said, "One of the dogs at the Humane Society is really special."

"It beats me," Wayne said, "why you want to hang around with a bunch of stray mutts. Next thing we know you'll have fleas."

"I like dogs," Kit said. "And Lynnette says sometimes the mixed breeds are smarter than the purebreds."

"Dogs," said Wayne, "are nothing but trouble. All they do is chew the furniture and wet on the carpets."

"Not when they're trained," Kit said. "This one . . ."

"Forget it," Wayne said. "We aren't getting a puppy."

"The one I'm talking about is two years old," Kit said. "Her puppy days are over. And she's smart. I know she'd be easy to house train. She might even be trained already."

"The last thing your mother needs is a dog to worry about."

Kit looked at Dorothy, hoping Dorothy would speak up in favor of Lady. Dorothy said nothing.

"You wouldn't have to worry about it," Kit said. "I'd feed Lady and take her out for walks every day before school and again when I get home. She could sleep in my room and stay there when I'm not home."

"Well . . ." Dorothy said.

"No," Wayne said.

"Wouldn't you at least think about it? She's really a nice dog and . . ."

79

"I said NO," Wayne said, "and that's the end of it."

"But . . ."

"You heard your father," Dorothy said.

Kit glared at Wayne. "He isn't," she said, "my father." She stood up and walked out of the room.

Why did they treat her like she was seven years old?

If Wayne wasn't so set against it, Dorothy would have agreed to give Lady a chance. Why was Dorothy's spine made of melted Jell-O?

She sat on her bed, pounding her fist rhythmically into her pillow. They wouldn't even let her tell them about Lady. It made no difference to them that Lady had been at The Humane Society a long time and if nobody adopted her soon, she would be euthanized. Lady was a gentle, calm dog. She wouldn't cause any trouble. If they would only give Lady a chance, Kit was sure they'd change their minds about her.

Kit put her head down on her knees. Sometimes she felt just as trapped as the unwanted dogs.

CHAPTER
9

W E'LL begin with Act Two,"
Miss Fenton said. "Berenice and John Henry: on stage, please.
Frankie, be ready for your entrance. Everyone else, QUIET."

There was a brief flurry as everyone moved into place.

Kit watched from the back of the auditorium. It was the
first rehearsal she had attended, although Tracy had urged her
repeatedly to come. Kit said she was volunteering at The Humane Society or baby-sitting every afternoon. She came now
because Justin, the school photographer, was going to take
pictures for the posters. She couldn't very well supervise the
pictures without being there.

"Curtain!" called Miss Fenton, even though they weren't
really using the curtain for rehearsals.

As Kit watched and listened, she was quickly caught up in
the characters and their words. Marcia no longer sounded like

Marcia. Her voice was higher, with a slight Southern accent. She no longer looked like Marcia, either. It wasn't just because she had exchanged her jeans and top for a short, shapeless cotton dress; it was the way she stood and moved. She seemed thinner, younger, more vulnerable. She was a forlorn, mixed-up twelve-year-old girl, who truly believed that her brother and his fiancée would want her to go along on their honeymoon.

Everyone knew their lines and knew when and where they were supposed to move.

"Pace," yelled Miss Fenton. "It's dragging. Pick up the pace!"

The actors spoke faster. Marcia's good, Kit thought. She's really good. So were the others. It was going to be a fabulous play.

When Act Two ended, Miss Fenton said, "We'll take a break now for some publicity photos. Please stay seated in the front rows while Kit explains what shots she wants, and then pose quickly. We still have to do all of Act Three today."

Kit had made a list of the scenes she wanted Justin to shoot. "First is the scene from Act One," she said, "with Frankie, Helen, and Doris."

Tracy and the girl who played Helen joined Marcia on stage and Kit told them where to stand. She put Marcia's back to the camera, so that Tracy's face showed.

"Thanks," Tracy whispered, after Justin took the picture. "You'll make me a star yet."

Kit continued down her list of pictures, including one of Miss Fenton holding her clipboard and talking with several cast members. All of the pictures Kit had planned were group shots, with at least three actors in each. Everyone cooperated. Nobody goofed off. Even Marcia kept quiet. There was a unity of spirit; the entire cast was willing to do whatever was necessary to make the publicity photos as good as possible.

Impulsively, Kit added one more shot to her list. "Last, I want one of Frankie by herself," she said.

Marcia stood alone on the stage.

"Give her a line, someone," Miss Fenton suggested. "Lead her into a scene."

From the front row, the others began saying their lines. When John Henry said, "You want me to get the weekend bag?" Marcia began to speak.

FRANKIE   *Don't bother me, John Henry. I'm thinking.*
JOHN HENRY   *What you thinking about?*
FRANKIE   *About the wedding. About my brother and the bride. Everything's been so sudden today. I never believed before about the fact that the earth turns at the rate of about a thousand miles a day. I didn't understand why it was that if you jumped up in the air you wouldn't land in Selma or Fairview or somewhere else instead of the same backyard. But now it seems to me I feel the world going around very fast.*

Marcia stretched out her arms and turned slowly in a circle. When she stopped, she looked at Justin and Kit as if she didn't see them. Her head tilted back; her eyes glittered in her pinched face. *I feel it turning and it makes me dizzy.*

Click. Justin's camera recorded the moment with a flash of light. Marcia blinked and dropped her arms.

"Thank you," Kit said. "You are a fantastic Frankie."

Justin left but Kit stayed to watch the rest of rehearsal. Tracy sat with her, since she only appeared in Act One.

When it was over, Miss Fenton gave comments on lines that she wanted the actors to do differently. Then she said, "There are a few props that the props committee hasn't been able to find. We still need a palmetto fan and we need a tape recording of a piano being tuned. Can any of you help?"

"I'll get them," Kit said. She had no idea where she would come up with either of the desired items but she suddenly wanted to volunteer, to have more of a part in making the play a success.

From then on, Kit went to play practice on the days when she didn't go to The Humane Society. She borrowed an old fan from an antique shop. She looked up Piano Tuners in the Yellow Pages, called the first name on the list, and explained what she needed. The tuner graciously agreed to help.

It was fun tracking down the needed props and when she brought them to rehearsal, Miss Fenton got as excited as if they were valuable works of art.

Tracy became Harriet Headline. "PROP GIRL FIRST FEMALE TO BE KNIGHTED BY QUEEN," she said. "ARMOR ORDERED."

Sharon Shocker responded, "PRODUCER IN AUDIENCE SMITTEN WITH 'DORIS'. ACTRESS OFFERED BROADWAY CONTRACT."

"Oh, sure," Tracy said. "He'll be smitten by all four of my lines."

As Kit joked with Tracy, she felt the tension between them dissolve. Her secret problem wasn't going to cost her Tracy's friendship, after all.

The next day in speech class, someone gave a talk on astrology, which led to a discussion of birth dates. When Miss Fenton said her birthday was the following Thursday, Kit decided to organize a surprise party. She talked to all of the cast and crew and everyone chipped in money for pizza, to be delivered immediately after rehearsal.

The two boys who were running lights volunteered to bring soft drinks and Kit decided to bake a chocolate birthday cake. Tracy spent the night with her, to help decorate it. With yellow frosting, they drew klieg lights and stars. Then they wrote, "Happy Birthday, Miss Fenton. Break a Leg!!"

"Fit for a king," Tracy declared, as they admired their masterpiece.

"TEENS OPEN BAKERY," Kit said. "BUCKINGHAM PALACE PLACES DAILY DESSERT ORDER."

On party day, rehearsal seemed to drag. Backstage, Kit and Tracy set out birthday napkins and paper cups.

"What if she's in a hurry to leave?" Tracy said. "Maybe she's going out to dinner with her boyfriend."

The stage manager looked startled. "She has a boyfriend?" he said. From his tone, Tracy might have suggested that Miss Fenton was dining with a giraffe.

"I don't know if she has a boyfriend or not," Tracy said, "but she probably does have plans for her birthday. Maybe her parents are having a family dinner."

"We should have fixed up a fake appointment with one of the other teachers," Kit said, "to be sure she can stay for the party." Why did she always realize what she should have done after it was too late?

The rest of the kids thought the cake was wonderful. Still,

Kit got more and more nervous By the time the pizza arrived, she was sure that Miss Fenton would not have time to eat it and would rush off without ever laying eyes on the masterpiece cake.

As soon as Act Three ended, everyone crowded into the green room, whispering excitedly. When Miss Fenton came to see what they were doing, they all shouted, "Surprise! Surprise!"

They sang, "Happy birthday to you," and Kit could tell that Miss Fenton was genuinely touched. When the song ended, Miss Fenton said, "Thank you, all of you."

"It was Kit's idea," Tracy said.

Kit quickly said, "Everyone helped." Then she added, "We hope you don't already have plans for dinner."

"None. And I can't think of anything I'd rather do than eat pizza with my favorite students."

Later, as they ate, Miss Fenton told Kit, "It takes time and effort to organize a party. I'm grateful."

"It was fun," Kit said. It *had* been fun but it was true that it took a lot of time.

Kit thought of all the birthday parties she had when she was small. Never anything unusual, like Tracy's parties, but Kit and her friends used to play drop-the-clothespin-in-the-bottle and musical chairs. Once a year, Dorothy even put aside her feelings about sweets and served birthday cake and ice cream.

Kit felt a rush of gratitude. Despite the gifts of hand lotion and underwear, Dorothy had always made Kit's birthdays special.

CHAPTER
10

KIT stared at the chart. She hadn't noticed it on her other visits but this time she saw it right away, hanging on the wall, just inside The Humane Society entrance. It listed each month of the current year and told how many dogs were taken in, how many were adopted and how many were euthanized. Then it gave the same statistics for cats.

It did not take a mental giant to figure out that in most months, only about half of the animals found homes. Some months, less than 50 percent of the dogs that were brought to The Humane Society were ever adopted, and the cats fared even worse.

She felt sick to her stomach.

"Sad, isn't it?" a voice behind her said.

Turning, Kit saw Mr. Morrison.

"It isn't right," she said. "Most of those animals are young and healthy. It isn't right to kill them."

"Heavens, girl, of course it isn't right. But what choice is there? They're kept here as long as there's room; eventually, they have to give up their space to incoming animals."

Kit looked again at the chart. March: 78 dogs euthanized. April: 61 dogs euthanized. In her mind, she saw a large furry heap of dead bodies. She shuddered.

She felt Mr. Morrison's hand on her shoulder. "When they die here, it is a peaceful and painless death," he said. "It's better than being hit by a car. It's better than starving or freezing. And it's better than being ravaged by wild animals or abused by humans. The animals here are treated kindly and their lives end with love, not fear."

Kit did not trust herself to speak.

Mr. Morrison handed her a leash. "I didn't come here to stand about and lecture," he said. "Come, girl. Let's take a couple of cage-mates out for some exercise. We can't control their future but we can make them happy today."

A few minutes later, they sat together on the picnic bench in the exercise yard while two dogs chased each other around.

"How long have you been a volunteer?" Kit asked.

"I've come twice a week for fifteen years. It's as good a place as any to practice the harmonica."

"Have you ever wanted to adopt one of the animals?"

"Heavens, girl, do you think I have no heart? Of course I want to adopt them. Right now, I wish I could take Sammy, the little gray schnauzer. Last month, it was a white and brown pointer named Maxine."

"Why don't you do it?"

"I can't. My wife's allergic to all animal fur. When I get home from here, I have to wash my clothes and take a shower right away."

"I wish I could adopt Lady," Kit said.

"The little terrier in the last cage?"

Kit nodded. "But my parents won't let me have a dog." Bitterness put a harsh edge on her voice.

"Then you're wise to help here. It's the next best thing." He glanced sideways at Kit. "And it beats sitting home feeling sorry for yourself. If you can't save the forest, plant a tree." He took the harmonica out of his pocket and began to play, "Summertime."

Kit threw two tennis balls and the dogs galloped after them. She didn't tell Mr. Morrison that she wasn't wise at all. She was at The Humane Society because she had to be.

When he finished his song he said, "Some day you'll be on your own, girl. You can have a dog then. You can have as many dogs as you want." He grinned at her. "Just don't marry someone who's allergic."

That day, she and Mr. Morrison worked together, exercising all the dogs that shared a cage. Once, after Kit coaxed a frightened poodle to play, Mr. Morrison said, "You have a way with animals, Kit. A gentleness that they respond to."

She smiled, pleased at the praise.

"They can tell, you know," he said. "Animals can tell whether a person is kind or not. They know if you like them or if you're pretending. They sense the truth about us humans, no matter how we might try to hide it."

"I do like the animals," Kit said. "They're so . . . straightforward."

He laughed. "A good description," he said. "I've yet to meet a deceitful dog. The truth is, I like most animals better than I like most people. Present company excepted, of course."

"Of course."

She had never met anyone like Mr. Morrison. He looked at least seventy, yet he treated Kit like an equal, as if the difference in their ages didn't matter to him.

As they leashed the last set of cage-mates and started back to the kennel, Mr. Morrison said, "It's time for these old bones to sit. I wouldn't want to disappoint any dogs who have been waiting for their concert." He took his campstool to the kennel and positioned it in the center of the walkway.

"I'm going to play with Lady for awhile before I leave," Kit said.

Mr. Morrison began a rousing chorus of "Beer Barrel Polka," while Kit got Lady. As she walked toward the door, with Lady trotting at her side, Mr. Morrison stopped in the middle of his tune.

"Ah, Kit. Look there, girl," he said, pointing at Lady. "You've earned the love light."

Puzzled, Kit looked at Lady. "What light?" she said.

"In her eyes, girl. In her eyes. See how her expression changes when she looks at you? It's the love light shining from within." He played a few random notes on the harmonica. "Lucky we are when we're seen through the light of love," he said, "be it shining in the eyes of human or beast. Some folks go all their days without ever seeing it directed at them. It's a splendid, special look. Cherish it."

He began playing, "Sweet Sixteen," and Kit hummed along as she led Lady out to the exercise yard.

As Kit played with Lady, she paid careful attention to the way Lady looked at her. Mr. Morrison was right. Lady's whole face seemed to glow from within whenever Kit spoke to her. The love light was indeed a splendid, special look.

That night, she told Tracy about Lady and about what Mr. Morrison had said. Tracy had come over to do homework together, but as usual, they spent most of the time talking about other things.

When Kit tried to explain the love light, Tracy nodded. "I know exactly what you mean," she said. "I never heard it called that before, but I've seen it."

"You have? Where? Who?"

"When my cousin got married. I got chills up my arms when I saw how he and his bride looked at each other. It was so— so adoring. Like they'd love each other always, no matter what happened."

"You sound like Frankie," Kit said.

"You're right. I didn't think of it until now but at my cousin's wedding, I saw what Frankie sees in the play. Love light."

"It's beautiful," Kit said. "And it's exactly the way Lady looks at me."

"Personally, I'd rather see some love light in the eyes of a tall, dark and handsome young man," Tracy said, "but if you can't have that, a dog will do."

"Lady is such a sweet dog," Kit said. "It just breaks my heart to see how she looks at me when I leave."

"I'm really proud of you for volunteering there," Tracy said. "It must be awful to see all the unwanted dogs and cats in cages. I don't think I could do it. No wonder they love you."

Before Kit could respond, Tracy jumped up and cried, "Oh, I can't stand it! I have to tell you!"

"Tell me what?"

"I am so proud of you for volunteering that I did something about it." She assumed her Harriet Headline voice. "HONORS HEAPED ON UNSELFISH GIRL," she cried. "POPE GRANTS SAINTHOOD."

Apprehension flitted on the edges of Kit's mind. "What do you mean?" she said. "What did you do?"

Tracy's eyes danced and she spoke slowly, as if she wanted to drag out the suspense.

"You know the Good Citizen Award at school? The one they give at Awards Night on the last day of school, when they give the Ninth Grade Scholarship and the sports letters and all?"

Kit nodded warily while her insides rollercoastered.

"You might get it." Tracy beamed, looking as if she would explode at any minute if she didn't get to tell more.

"Me? Why would I get it?"

"Because I nominated you." Tracy plunked down on the edge of Kit's bed. "I saw the nomination blanks in the school office. It was the same day you told me you were going to do volunteer work with homeless animals and I thought, if anybody deserves a Good Citizen Award, it's Kit. So I put down why I was nominating you and today in the mail, there was a letter saying that you are one of the finalists."

Triumphantly, Tracy whisked the letter from her purse and thrust it at Kit.

Kit opened it and began to read. *We are happy to inform you that your nominee, Kit Hathaway, has been chosen as a*

92

finalist for the Good Citizen of the Year Award. We agree that her volunteer work at The Humane Society is worthy of recognition. The winner will be announced . . .

Kit quit reading and looked at Tracy. She was serving a sentence for shoplifting; she couldn't possibly accept any kind of award for volunteer work.

"Even if you don't win, you'll get an Honorable Mention certificate, for being a finalist. Isn't that great?"

Slowly, Kit handed the letter back to Tracy. "I can't accept any award," Kit said. "You'll have to withdraw my nomination."

Tracy looked at Kit as if she'd just sprouted whiskers. "What are you talking about? Why can't you accept it?"

"I just can't." Kit looked down at the floor. "You shouldn't have nominated me without telling me."

"I wanted to surprise you," Tracy said. "I thought you'd be glad. I thought . . ."

"I'm sorry," Kit said. "I know you were trying to do something nice for me and I appreciate that but I can't be a finalist for the Good Citizen Award."

There was a long silence. Too long. Kit continued to inspect the floor.

"What's wrong?" Tracy said.

"Nothing's wrong."

"Don't give me that. There has to be a reason why you want me to withdraw your name."

"Because I don't deserve the award."

"The committee will decide that. Obviously, they think you *are* deserving, or you wouldn't be a finalist."

Kit got up and walked to the window. She was not a true

93

volunteer. The award should go to someone who was helping because she wanted to help, not to someone who had been ordered to help by the Juvenile Court Committee.

But she couldn't explain that unless she told Tracy about the shoplifting. It would have been bad enough to tell Tracy when it happened. It would be even worse now, after she'd already worked out a way to have it disappear from her record. She would never have to tell anyone at all.

"I can't explain it to you," Kit said.

"First it was my party. Now this. What's going on with you?"

"Nothing."

"I know you better than that. Something is wrong." Tracy's voice dropped almost to a whisper. "We've never kept secrets from each other," she said. "Whatever it is that's wrong, you know I'd be on your side."

Kit was tempted. It would be such a relief not to pretend anymore, not to keep hiding the truth from Tracy.

"Remember the TRIK Club?" Tracy said. "When we vowed to be friends forever?"

I remember. And we also vowed to be honest and good. No loyal member of the TRIK Club would ever shoplift.

"I can't tell you."

Tracy looked at her for a long moment. Then she shrugged and said, "OK. OK, I'll withdraw your name." She put the letter back in her purse and stood up.

"Thanks, anyway," Kit said.

"Sure."

A few minutes earlier, they had been chattering like crows

94

in a cornfield. Now there didn't seem to be anything else to say.

After Tracy left, Kit stood at the window for a long time, looking for stars in the black sky. Had she done the right thing? She knew it was right to withdraw her name, but had she been right not to tell Tracy the reason?

She didn't like keeping a secret from Tracy. She and Tracy had been best friends since second grade, when they discovered a mutual love of peanut butter and banana sandwiches. Tracy had always been there for Kit, had always understood Kit's moods. Tracy was the only one who knew about Wayne's binges and about the Triple-B Treatment and about Kit's hopes for the Ninth Grade Scholarship.

Was that why Tracy had nominated Kit? Maybe she suspected that Marcia Homer had the best chance for the scholarship now, because of the play. Maybe she was using the Good Citizen Award as a way to boost Kit's chances for the scholarship. If so, she needn't have bothered. With Miss Fenton on the court committee, Kit knew there was no way she could win the scholarship now.

Kit closed her eyes and took a deep breath. In the past, Tracy always made Kit feel good about herself because Tracy believed Kit was wonderful. Of course, Kit felt the same way about Tracy. Tracy *was* wonderful. She was fun and smart and cheerful. And unselfish. It was typical of Tracy to nominate Kit for an award, rather than trying to win something for herself.

A year ago, Kit would have been thrilled with Tracy's nomination. Now it made her feel guilty because, in addition to

Tracy's other good qualities, Tracy was honest. Kit was sure Tracy would never steal anything.

And that's why I can't tell her, Kit thought. I don't want her to know what I did because she would think less of me and I want her always to think I'm wonderful.

Even if I'm not.

CHAPTER 11

FREE to Good Home: "LADY"
Small Friendly Dog. Terrier mix. 2 years old.

KIT added her name, home-
room, and phone number before she tacked the notice on the
bulletin board in the school cafeteria. She had decided to pay
Lady's adoption fee, even if she didn't get to keep Lady herself;
it might help Lady get adopted. Maybe someone Kit knew
would take Lady and Kit could go visit her sometimes.

As she stepped back to make sure her printing was big
enough to attract attention, she saw Tracy approaching. Kit
pointed to her notice.

"I had this idea after you left last night," she said. "Maybe if I pay the fee out of my baby-sitting money, Lady will have a better chance."

Tracy just looked at her.

"I'd rather have Lady myself, but a home with someone else is better than no home at all."

Tracy was silent.

"I figure the word FREE will at least attract some interest. All I have to do is get somebody to look at Lady and from then on, she'll sell herself."

When Tracy still said nothing, Sharon Shocker pretended to read from a newspaper. "PHILANTHROPIST OFFERS RARE, VALUABLE DOG TO PUBLIC."

Tracy didn't laugh.

"What's the matter? Don't you think it's a good idea?"

"I think it's a great idea," Tracy said. Her tone of voice didn't match her words.

"What's wrong?" Kit said.

"That's what I'd like to know. Here you are, offering to use your own money to pay the fee so somebody else can adopt a dog but you won't let me nominate you for the Good Citizen Award. It doesn't makes sense, Kit. Won't you reconsider? I haven't withdrawn your name yet; it isn't too late to change your mind."

"I can't change my mind." As Tracy looked at her, Kit felt a distance between them, an awkwardness that had never been there before. She knew that Tracy still hoped Kit might confide the reason why she had refused the Good Citizen nomination.

She imagined the headline. "BRAINLESS WONDER ARRESTED FOR SHOPLIFTING. FAMILY DISGRACED. FRIEND HORRIFIED." No, Kit corrected. Make that "EX-FRIEND."

They walked in silence the rest of the way to class.

When they got to speech class, Miss Fenton held up a glass fishbowl filled with slips of paper. "Instead of a final test in this class," she said, "you will each give a major speech, one which will require some original research."

Immediately, Arthur asked, "What's the difference between original research and unoriginal research?"

His buddy, Phil, said, "Unoriginal research is when you copy my notes." Both boys snickered.

"Original research," Miss Fenton said, "means facts that haven't been published. Instead of looking only in the library for information, you will have to talk to people. Do an interview. Gather ideas and opinions on your own." Miss Fenton nodded toward the fishbowl. "I've chosen a variety of topics and put each one on a piece of paper. You will draw the topics at random."

A few kids groaned and started to complain but the plan sounded fair to Kit. She had noticed that some people always balk at new ideas. They're suspicious of anything different, no matter how good it might be.

Miss Fenton ignored the complaints. Instead she held up the fishbowl and looked directly at the class. A boy in the front row got up, reached in, and selected a topic for his speech.

Kit looked at Tracy. Tracy gave a little nod. They went to the front of the room, put their hands in the fishbowl and each took a piece of paper.

Kit opened hers on the way back to her desk. She stopped in the middle of the aisle and stared at the paper in her hand. TEENAGE SHOPLIFTING. Was this Miss Fenton's idea of a joke? Had she planned it so Kit would draw this topic?

She turned and looked at her teacher but Miss Fenton was not watching Kit; she was holding the fishbowl while two other students selected their topics.

I can't do it, Kit thought. I cannot stand in front of the class and give a speech on shoplifting. I'd be a nervous wreck. I'll stay after class and ask if I can trade this topic for a different one.

"Look what I got," Tracy said. She handed her paper to Kit and Kit read the words, SIBLING RIVALRY. "Now, how am I supposed to know anything about sibling rivalry," Tracy said, "when I'm an only child?"

"Research," Kit said. "Original research."

"What did you get?" Tracy held out her hand for Kit's topic.

Kit hesitated. If she showed it to Tracy, she couldn't ask for a different topic. If she refused to show it to Tracy, Tracy would wonder why, and Kit would never be able to explain. She couldn't have another obvious secret from Tracy. That would be too much.

Slowly, she handed the paper to Tracy.

Tracy looked at Kit's paper. "That makes me feel better," she said. "You don't know any more about shoplifting than I know about sibling rivalry."

Kit said nothing.

"My cousin, Glorie, could talk about shoplifting," Tracy said. "When Glorie was invited to join the Ace Club at her school, part of the initiation was that she had to shoplift something from Sears. All the other club members waited outside, in the parking lot, and Glorie had to go in and swipe something and bring it to them."

"What did she take?"

"A scarf. She said she was scared to death but she just stuck it in her coat pocket and walked out with it."

"Nobody stopped her?"

"She said there was nothing to it. She never wore the scarf, though. She was afraid her mother would ask her where she got it and if her folks ever found out she stole it, they'd kill her."

Nothing to it, Kit thought. Right. Maybe it was easy for Glorie, but it sure as heck wasn't easy for me.

"I told Glorie she was nuts to do it," Tracy said. "What if she'd been caught? She could end up in Juvenile Court over a stupid scarf that she didn't even want."

"What did she say?"

"She said she wanted to be an Ace." Tracy rolled her eyes. "Glorie never did have the brains of a flea. And it turned out that she didn't get to be an Ace, anyway. The initiation was really a test of honesty. If Glorie had refused to take something from Sears, she would have been in the club. Because she took the scarf, she wasn't."

Tracy glanced again at her own topic. "There's one good thing about sibling rivalry," she said. "I can just interview kids I know. You'll probably have to talk to a police officer or the security guard at one of the stores."

Kit shivered. Just the thought made her blood turn cold.

That afternoon, Kit picked up the photographs that were taken during rehearsal. She had to choose which one to have enlarged and reproduced for the big posters that would go in store windows.

The one of Tracy's scene was good but the one of Marcia alone was best. The expression on her face captured the essence of the play.

Kit never hesitated. She chose Marcia's picture for the main posters. Marcia might have a big mouth but she was a good actress and she deserved to have her picture on the posters.

Kit decided to use the other photos for smaller signs around the school. When she got home, she spread all of her art materials out on the living room floor and experimented with different layouts for the signs. She glued the photo of Tracy to a large piece of red construction paper and began lettering in the name of the play.

She concentrated so hard that she didn't hear the telephone ring, nor did she hear Wayne answer it. She didn't know about the call until he began yelling.

"What the hell is going on?" Wayne hollered from the kitchen. "Dorothy! Kit! Damn it all, where is everybody?"

Now what, Kit thought.

"I'm right here," Dorothy called, as she hurried down the stairs. "What's the matter?"

Wayne stormed into the living room. "That phone call was an attorney for Pierre's," he yelled. "She said we owe them three hundred dollars and they're going to sue us if we don't pay."

"Calm down," Dorothy said. "It isn't good to get so angry. You'll have a heart attack."

Kit slowly put down her colored markers and looked at Wayne. His face was flushed. He stood beside her, glaring down at her.

"The attorney said Kit was shoplifting," he said. "The store claims we owe three hundred dollars for civil restitution. She said she sent a letter and a bill. If it isn't paid by next Monday, they're taking us to small claims court." He ran his hand nervously across his head.

Kit could tell from the look on Dorothy's face that she had received the letter and the bill. She always read the mail first; it would be easy for Dorothy to keep the letter a secret from Wayne. But why didn't she show it to Kit? Did she think Pierre's didn't really mean what they said?

"Now, Wayne," Dorothy said, "I can explain."

"I don't want explanations," Wayne thundered. "I only want to know one thing. Is this true? Was Kit stealing? Because if she was, I'm going to . . ." He stopped, as if unable to think of any punishment worthy of the crime.

"I'm sure we can straighten this out," Dorothy said.

"IS IT TRUE OR NOT?"

Kit stood up and faced him. "Yes," she said. "It's true."

The blood seemed to drain from Wayne's face. "What did you steal?" he asked.

"A gold bracelet."

"She gave it back," Dorothy said.

"Why wasn't I told?" Wayne said.

"It happened while you were—sick," Dorothy said. "We didn't want to upset you. I was going to send them the three hundred dollars, as soon as I had it."

Wayne took a step closer to Kit. "Why would you steal a bracelet? What's the matter with you?"

"It won't happen again," Kit said.

"Why did you do it?"

"I don't know."

103

She expected him to yell some more. She was sure he would take away TV privileges or cut her allowance. Instead, Wayne turned slowly away from her, sank down on the couch, and put his head in his hands.

"Shoplifting." That's all he said. Just one word. Somehow it was worse than if he'd yelled.

"What do they mean by *civil restitution*?" Dorothy said. "Do we have to pay for the security guard's time?"

"The attorney said civil restitution is a legal way to help retail stores get back part of what they lose to shoplifters," Wayne said. "And we're responsible. As her parents, we're responsible for what she does and we have to pay the bill."

"She didn't mean to steal. It just—happened." Dorothy sat beside him and put her hand on his shoulder. "It won't go on her record," she said. "She has to do community service—that's why she goes to The Humane Society—and as soon as she's put in enough hours, the whole thing gets dropped. It's all erased, just as if it had never happened."

It might be erased from the official record, Kit thought, but it wasn't going to be so easy to erase it from her life. Whether the charge was dropped by the court or not, she knew it was going to haunt her for a long, long time.

CHAPTER
12

KIT emptied all the money from her bank and counted it. Sixty-six dollars and twenty-five cents. It had seemed like a fortune the last time she counted. Now it was pitifully small, compared to what she owed.

She put forty-five dollars back in the bank, to be used in case someone at school agreed to adopt Lady. Wayne could wait awhile to get his money; Lady needed help right now.

She took a piece of notebook paper and began to write.

Dear Wayne:
   I'm sorry.
   I wish I had never taken the bracelet and I'd give anything if I could undo all the trouble. I will repay the $300 with my baby-sitting money. Here is $21.25. It's all I have right now but I'll get the rest as soon as I can.

$300.00
－21.25
$278.75 Balance due

Kit signed her name, folded the letter, and put it in an envelope. Then she put the $21.25 in the envelope, too. Since she had only one dollar bills, she could barely get the bulging envelope sealed.

She thought about all the hours of baby-sitting that the money represented: changing Willy Klompton's diapers, playing endless games of "Go Fish" with Jennifer Peters, washing two days' worth of dirty dishes for Mrs. Klompton, who always left her kitchen in a shambles and then asked Kit to, "tidy up a bit, after the baby's asleep."

Kit sighed, taped the envelope shut, and went downstairs.

Wayne and Dorothy were watching television. Kit knew she could have talked to them, instead of writing the letter, but it seemed better to do it in writing. More official. She waited until a commercial break, so she was sure to have their attention. Then she handed the envelope to Wayne.

"This is for you," she said.

He opened the envelope and removed the contents. He looked surprised but he said nothing. He just began counting the bills. Dorothy reached for Kit's note and read it.

Typical Wayne, Kit thought. He doesn't care what I have to say; he only cares about the money.

She turned and left the room. As she did, she heard Dorothy say, "She's going to pay you back. Every dime."

Kit went to her room and rummaged in her desk drawer for the partial bag of chocolate stars that she'd stashed there. She got her current library book from the table beside her bed, locked herself in the bathroom, and filled the tub. Maybe the Triple-B Treatment would help her forget how many hours of Mrs. Klompton's dirty dishes and Willy Klompton's dirty diapers it was going to take to earn $278.75.

The next day, Kit went to school filled with hope. Two boys had talked with her about adopting Lady. Both had promised to speak to their parents and let Kit know if they could have a dog. Surely, Kit thought, one of them would be able to take Lady.

She hurried to her locker, hoping that one of the boys would be waiting for her. Instead, Marcia Homer was there, talking to Tracy.

"Kit!" Marcia cried. "I have wonderful news. My parents said I can have your dog."

"You? You can?" Kit stammered.

She felt Tracy's hand on her arm.

"I saw the notice yesterday," Marcia said, "and as soon as I got home from play rehearsal I talked to Mom and she said it was OK with her if it was OK with Daddy, but he had a meeting last night and didn't get home until late so I couldn't call you." Marcia twirled in a circle, hugging herself. "We used to have a dog," she said, "but he got sick and we had to have him put to sleep. When I told Mom about your dog, she said she's missed having Friskie underfoot. She said we can come over to your house after play rehearsal today and if we like Lady, we'll take her right then."

Kit licked her lips, trying to sort out her thoughts. "She isn't at my house," Kit said. "She's at The Humane Society."

"She isn't your dog? I thought . . ."

"I help at The Humane Society and Lady's such a nice dog that I'm trying to find a home for her."

Marcia thought about that for a moment. "Are you sure she's a friendly dog? And healthy?"

"Positive."

"Well, then I guess it doesn't make any difference whether she's yours or not," Marcia said. "Where is The Humane Society?"

Kit gave Marcia directions and they agreed to meet there at 4:30.

When Marcia left, Tracy exploded. "Of all the people in the school," she said, "why would it have to be Marcia?"

Kit could only shake her head.

"How much is the adoption fee?" Tracy asked.

"Forty-five dollars. It includes her shots and being spayed."

Tracy groaned. "Forty-five hard-earned dollars. All for someone who already has more money than she needs."

"It's OK," Kit said. "Marcia's spoiled and she brags too much but a home is a home. Lady will get plenty to eat and lots of attention." She thought of how Lady always wagged her tail whenever Kit talked to her. "She'll probably even like listening to Marcia."

Tracy rolled her eyes. "I thought you said the dog was smart," she said.

Kit hurried home after school, got the forty-five dollars from her bank, and took the bus to The Humane Society. She wanted to arrive well before Marcia and her mother got there, to have some time with Lady by herself. She had a comb in her pocket, and a red ribbon. She wanted Lady to look her best.

Kit had already decided that she wouldn't visit Lady at

Marcia's house. It would be more than she could stand. She would play with Lady today and not see her again.

Lynnette was talking on the phone when Kit arrived, so she went straight to the kennel. She walked toward the back, stopping to say a few words to each dog and letting them sniff her fingers through the wire cage doors.

When she reached the last cage, she stopped. A black and tan Doberman lunged at the door of the cage.

Quickly, Kit looked at the paper that was clipped to the cage door. *Jasper. Part Doberman. 9 months old. Owner moved to an apartment that doesn't allow dogs.* The paper was dated the day before.

There was no paper for Lady. Kit's notes, carefully recording the times when she had socialized Lady, were gone. Lady was gone, too.

Quickly, Kit strode back through the kennel, peering carefully at each cage, just in case Lady had been moved. There was no reddish-gold terrier.

No velvety ears. No love light. No Lady.

Kit's heart pounded in her ears as she ran out of the kennel and across the yard to the office. She crossed her fingers as she ran. Maybe the family of her daydreams had adopted Lady. Maybe Lady, right at that very moment, was romping in her own fenced yard, fresh from a bath. Maybe a little child was hugging her and feeding her dog treats.

Or maybe . . .

CHAPTER
13

KIT had to know.

She rapped quickly on the open door to Lynnette's office and then, without waiting for Lynnette to say hello, Kit blurted it out.

"Where's Lady?"

"Lady?"

"Yes. Before, she was always in the very last cage. She isn't there today. What happened to her?"

"The little terrier."

"Yes. What happened to her?"

Lynnette got up, walked around her desk, and closed the office door. "Sit down, Kit."

Kit knew. Lady wasn't playing with her new family. Lady wasn't running in the grass or getting her tummy rubbed or eating dog treats. Even before Lynnette told her, Kit knew that

Lady had become one of the terrible statistics on the chart, one of the 50 percent that doesn't get chosen.

"I'm sorry," Lynnette said. "We kept her as long as we could."

"She was such a nice dog," Kit said.

Lynnette nodded. "Most of them are."

"I found someone who said they might take her," Kit said. "They're coming this afternoon."

"Oh, Kit," Lynnette said. "We didn't know that."

"I wanted her myself. I tried . . ." Her voice broke and she stopped talking, struggling for control.

"Go ahead and cry," Lynette said. "This has happened to all of us who work here."

"How do you stand it?" Kit sobbed.

Lynnette handed her a tissue. "If we weren't here, what would have happened to Lady?"

Kit thought about Lady, hungry and cold, dodging cars along the freeway.

"We gave her a chance," Lynnette said. "It didn't work for Lady, but it does for many of the animals. Each time, we hope it will. We gave Lady a chance, and you gave her love. You gave her exercise and attention and some happiness. Be glad of that."

"How can I be glad when Lady's dead?"

"You did what you could for her. So did I. We both wish we could have done more but at least we did something. We tried."

"She was only two years old. She would have lived a lot more years." Kit blew her nose. "It isn't fair," she said.

"No," Lynnette agreed. "It isn't."

Kit took a deep breath and stood up.

"I am sorry," Lynnette said. There were tears in her eyes as she spoke. "If you don't want to come back, I'll understand. I'll sign your report and give you credit for the full twenty hours. You've more than earned it."

As Kit opened the office door, she thought about what Lynnette had said and she knew it was true. She had done all she could for Lady. She had tried her best and despite the way it turned out, she was glad that she tried. Because of her, Lady had run in the yard and played ball and had her tummy rubbed. Because of her, Lady's tail had thumped and the love light had glowed in Lady's eyes.

She turned and looked at Lynnette. "I'll be back," she said. "I'll finish my time."

"I'm glad," Lynnette said.

"And when my twenty hours are up, I want to keep on coming. I'd like to be a volunteer, every week."

Lynnette put her arms around Kit and hugged her.

Marcia and Mrs. Homer arrived a few minutes later.

"The dog I told you about isn't here anymore," Kit said.

"She got adopted already?" Marcia said. "Oh, rats, I was afraid of that."

"Then we'll just look at the other dogs," Mrs. Homer said. "We're here now and we're all set to take a dog home. Maybe there's one we'll like even better."

Kit thought fast. "The others aren't free," she said.

"That doesn't matter," Mrs. Homer said.

"I'll show you where the kennels are," Kit said.

She watched while Marcia and her mother went from cage to cage. Marcia covered her ears and complained about the barking but Mrs. Homer seemed to feel sorry for the dogs. She stopped several times and let different ones sniff her fingers. When she came to a chubby tan dog, she clapped her hands, clearly delighted. Then she poked Marcia and pointed at the dog.

Kit knew the dog. It was Pansy, part cocker and part poodle. Kit had socialized Pansy on her last visit.

Kit got a leash, opened Pansy's cage, and led her out to the exercise yard. Marcia and Mrs. Homer followed, talking excitedly about how much Pansy looked like Friskie, the dog they used to have.

As she listened to them, Kit knew they were going to take Pansy home with them. "I'll let you get acquainted by yourselves," she said, as she handed the leash to Marcia. "If you decide you want her, just go in the office and they'll help you make the arrangements."

"I can't believe our good luck," Mrs. Homer said. "We came to look at a different dog and here's one that's exactly what we want."

"Even if Lady hadn't been adopted already, we'd want Pansy," Marcia said. "I can't wait to take her home and teach her to fetch."

"Tomorrow I'll take her to the groomers," Mrs. Homer said. "We'll get her hair trimmed and have her bathed."

"And put ribbons behind her ears," Marcia added.

"We'll need to buy a new doggie bed. Let's look for a flowered one this time."

"And toys!" Marcia said.

Mrs. Homer laughed. "Oh, yes. A ball and a chewbone so she doesn't ruin the furniture and maybe one of those soft squeaky toys for her to carry around. Remember how Friskie always liked those squeaky toys?"

It was like the night in Pierre's all over again. Kit watched and listened, overwhelmed with envy. Why couldn't Dorothy be more like Mrs. Homer?

As Kit walked back past the kennel, she heard harmonica music. Looking in, she saw Mr. Morrison sitting on his stool, playing a lively tune. When he saw her, he stopped playing and walked toward her.

"I heard your favorite pup got put down yesterday," he said. "I'm sorry, girl. I am, indeed."

"If only Wayne wasn't so selfish and my mother wasn't such a wimp," Kit said, "Lady would still be alive. She'd be at my house right now, waiting for me to come home and play with her."

"Don't waste your life on if-onlys," he said.

She scowled at him. She hoped he wasn't going to give her some kind of a sermon.

"The animals have no control over their lives," he said. "They can't reach through the wire and open their own cages. But we humans can."

"I could have set Lady free, if my mother had let me. But, no. She did what Wayne wanted. She always does what Wayne wants. Always!"

"Perhaps your mother is trapped, too."

"You just said people don't have to stay caged and you're right. My mother doesn't have to let Wayne control her. She has a choice."

"So do you, girl." He played a few haunting notes on his harmonica. Kit waited, not sure what he meant. "Don't let resentment and bitterness rob you of happiness," he said. "Unlike Lady, you can set yourself free."

Before Kit could respond, he turned away from her and went back in the kennel, playing "Somewhere Over the Rainbow" as he walked.

What does he know? Kit thought. He's just a foolish old man who plays music for dogs. How can he possibly know what would make me happy?

All the way home on the bus, Kit struggled to hold back her tears. She had come so close to finding a home for Lady. Kit leaned her forehead on the cool window and closed her eyes.

"Put to sleep." "Euthanized." "Put down." No matter what phrase was used to try to make the ugly reality prettier, it still came down to the same thing.

Lady was dead.

CHAPTER 14

KIT couldn't stop crying. She lay face down on her bed, choked with tears. She knew her eyes would be puffy and her nose would be red the next day. She knew that crying wouldn't do any good, yet she couldn't stop.

Lady's death unleashed all of Kit's pent-up feelings about anything bad that had ever happened. She cried because her stepfather drank too much and because she was sure Marcia would win the Ninth Grade Scholarship and because there were too many unwanted animals in the world. Most of all, she cried because everything she did seemed to go wrong.

After awhile, Dorothy stood tentatively in the doorway of Kit's room and asked Kit if she would like something to drink. Kit shook her head.

"Why don't you get up now?" Dorothy said. "You'll feel better if you splash cold water on your face."

Kit knew her mother was right but she shook her head again. She didn't want to feel better. Not yet.

She heard Wayne ask, "Is she still carrying on?"

"We should have taken the dog," Dorothy said. "I didn't know Lady would be . . . that this would happen. We should have let Kit bring her home."

"We can't take in every flea-bitten stray in the whole kennel."

"No. But she didn't ask to bring them all home; she only asked for one."

It was the first time Kit had ever heard Dorothy take her side against Wayne. Too bad she didn't do it sooner, when it would have done Lady some good.

"Well, it's too late now," Wayne said. He lowered his voice but Kit could still hear anyway. "It was only a dog, Dorothy. Some stray mutt. The way she's acting, you'd think it was one of us who died."

Kit clenched her teeth together and burrowed her face into her pillow to keep from saying something she shouldn't say. She heard Dorothy shushing Wayne as they left. "You don't mean that, Wayne."

Yes, he does, Kit thought. He means every word of it.

Half an hour later, there was a quick tap on her door. Tracy came in and stood beside Kit's bed. She held a bouquet of daffodils.

"I brought these for you," Tracy said. "I'm sorry about Lady."

"How did you find out?"

"Your mother called me and asked if I could come over for awhile. She said she thought you might like someone to talk to." She handed the flowers to Kit and sat beside her. "It's odd," she said. "This morning I was angry because Marcia was going to get the dog you wanted; now I'm angry because she *didn't* get Lady."

"Marcia took one of the other dogs," Kit said.

"Did you have to pay the fee?"

"No."

"Good. At least you still have your forty-five dollars. It would have bugged me if you had paid the fee for Marcia. Now you can do something fun with that money."

Kit didn't say so but she knew she wasn't going to do anything fun with her baby-sitting money for a long time. Every dime of it was going to Wayne until she had repaid the three hundred dollars.

"You know what your mother said, when she let me in just now? She looked at the daffodils and said she wished she'd thought of that. And Wayne agreed."

"Wayne said he wished he had bought me flowers? That'll be the day."

"I think Wayne wants to be friendly," Tracy said, "only he doesn't know how. I always feel as if he would like to talk to me but he isn't sure what to say."

"He said Lady was only a stray mongrel and he doesn't understand why I'm crying."

"That's what I mean. He's like somebody from another planet who has never seen people before. He really doesn't understand."

"Well, I don't understand him, either, so we're even." Kit

went in the bathroom and splashed cool water on her face, soothing her aching eyes. She looked in the mirror and quickly looked away. Her face was red and blotchy. She looked like she was fresh from another planet herself.

"I started my original research," Tracy said. "I talked to three people about their brothers and sisters. One girl told me that her brother used to collect spiders in a jar and turn them loose in her bedroom. I'll never complain again about being an only child."

Kit knew that Tracy was trying to cheer her up by changing the subject, but thinking about the speech she had to give on teenage shoplifting only made Kit feel worse. There was no way she was going to interview any store security people— just thinking about it made her stomach do cartwheels. Maybe she should try to talk to Tracy's cousin, Glorie. She didn't know any other teenaged shoplifters. Except herself.

The next afternoon during American History, two buzzers rang, alerting the class to a message on the intercom. The teacher waited.

"Please send Kit Hathaway to the office. Kit Hathaway to the office, please."

Everyone looked at Kit.

"Go ahead, Kit," the teacher said.

Kit got up and walked to the door. Why would she get called to the office?

When she got there, the school secretary said, "The principal wants to talk to you."

Puzzled, Kit turned toward Mrs. Dobson's office.

"I'm afraid I have some bad news," Mrs. Dobson said. "Your mother is in the hospital?"

"What happened? Was she in an accident?"

"I'm sorry, I don't have any details. Someone from Overview Hospital called me and asked me to give you the message. I called back, to verify that it wasn't a prank call. Your mother was admitted about an hour ago. She's in the emergency room." Mrs. Dobson opened a desk drawer and removed her purse. "I'll drive you there, if you like," she said.

"Yes. Thanks."

"You'd better get your coat and anything else you'll need. I'll wait here for you."

Kit hurried to her locker to get her things. She scribbled a quick note and stuck it through the slot in Tracy's locker. *Dorothy's in hospital. I'll call you later. K.*

When Mrs. Dobson and Kit got to the emergency room waiting area, Wayne was pacing the floor. She hurried over to him.

"What's wrong?" she asked.

"We don't know yet," Wayne said. "She called me at work. Said she was in terrible pain. By the time I got home, she was in bad shape. Pale and shaky and sweating. She couldn't even talk, to tell me what was wrong. We came straight to the hospital."

"Is there anything else I can do for you?" Mrs. Dobson asked, before she left.

"No," Wayne said. "Thank you for bringing Kit."

Wayne looked pale and shaky himself. "All I could think of in the car was that she's having a heart attack. That's how she looked to me, like she was having a heart attack." He gripped Kit's arm. "But how could that be?" he said. "How could Dorothy have a heart attack?"

Kit knew what he meant. Dorothy ran six miles almost every day, she was thin, she had never smoked. How could she have a heart attack when she did everything possible to prevent one?

Still, what if it *was* a heart attack? What if Dorothy died?

All of the times she had criticized Dorothy flashed through Kit's mind and she was overwhelmed with guilt. What a rotten daughter I've been, she thought. Maybe Dorothy isn't the perfect parent, but I could have worse. In her own way, she tries and what have I ever done for her?

As if he was thinking exactly the same thing, Wayne said, "If Dorothy makes it through this, let's try to get along better. It drives her nuts when we fight." Wayne's neck got red, as if it strained him to talk this way. "I'm not blaming you," he said. "I know I haven't been much of a father. I just don't know how to act or what to say."

"I haven't been the world's greatest daughter, either," Kit admitted.

"The trouble is," Wayne said, "Dorothy's the one who gets hurt. I get mad at you and you get mad at me but it's Dorothy who suffers. She's spent the last five years trying to make us like each other."

Kit knew he was right. She also knew that some doctors said stress can cause heart trouble. Was that what had happened to Dorothy? Was she so strung out because of Wayne and Kit that it had affected her health?

Kit didn't think things were that bad. Still, Dorothy did worry a lot and she spent a lot of time trying to smooth out the wrinkles between Kit and Wayne.

"You want to know something funny?" Wayne said. "One reason she married me is because she thought you needed a man in your life. A father. She said little girls always adore their fathers and she wanted you to have that relationship. How's that for a laugh? If she'd known what a failure I was going to be in the fatherhood department, she would never have said *yes*."

Kit looked at Wayne in astonishment. She had never heard him admit he was wrong about anything, much less call himself a failure. "I think she wanted to marry you for herself," she said, "not just for me."

Wayne stared down at the floor, as if he didn't hear her. "The worst part of all," he said, "is that I don't even know what I did wrong. If we could go back and start all over again, I'd probably make the same mistakes with you that I made the first time. Even if we got a second chance, you'd still end up hating me."

"I don't hate you," Kit said.

"It sure isn't love," he said.

A doctor approached them. "It's acute appendicitis," he said. "We're preparing her for surgery." He handed Wayne a clipboard with some papers on it. "I'll need your signature on these, Mr. Gillette. They give us permission for the surgery. Read them carefully and, after you've signed, give them to one of the nurses."

Wayne nodded and took the clipboard.

"We'll have some word for you as soon as we can." The doctor left, leaving Wayne and Kit alone in the waiting room.

Kit sat down and Wayne sat beside her. Together, they began reading the papers. When Kit got to the part about the risks of anesthesia, she stopped. "This sounds scary," she said. "Here, where it says unforeseen conditions may arise."

"I'll sign it," he said. "The hospital has to protect itself but if Dorothy needs surgery, that's what she'll get."

He took a pen from his shirt pocket and signed the papers. Then he got up and took them to one of the nurses.

When he returned, looking frightened, he sat beside Kit and put his head in his hands.

He loves her, too, Kit thought. And he's afraid he might lose her.

We finally have something in common. Wayne is just as scared as I am.

CHAPTER
15

It was a long afternoon. Wayne paced back and forth, unable to sit still for more than a minute at a time. Kit tried to read the *National Geographic* magazines that were in the waiting room but was unable to concentrate.

At 4:30, Tracy rushed in. "What happened?" she cried. "Is your mom OK?"

Glad for the distraction, Kit gave her the details.

"I'll wait with you," Tracy said.

"Don't you have play practice?"

"Miss Fenton excused me." She sat beside Kit. "Remember that time I broke my arm, and you tried to heal it by saying a magic chant? Something about a lizard tail?"

Kit smiled. Of course she remembered. It had taken her two hours to write that chant. In a low, spooky voice she said:

"Tail of lizard, drops of dew,
Make my mother good as new."

The word "new" was barely out of her mouth when the doctor appeared. "She's doing fine," he said. "We got the appendix before it ruptured and she'll be good as new in a few days."

Kit grabbed Tracy and hugged her. Then, impulsively, she hugged Wayne, too. He looked dumbfounded. He didn't hug her back but he mumbled, "Thanks."

Tracy, in her most melodramatic Harriet Headline voice, cried, "DAUGHTER'S MAGIC CHANT SAVES MOTHER! MAYO CLINIC RENAMED HATHAWAY HOSPITAL AFTER DOCTOR REVEALS MEDICAL MIRACLE!"

The doctor raised one eyebrow. "I beg your pardon?" he said.

Already giddy with relief, Kit shrieked with laughter. Wayne burst out laughing, too. As they guffawed together, Kit thought, maybe there's hope for us yet.

Kit didn't visit her mother the next afternoon because it was her day to work at The Humane Society. She was glad. Compared to people, the animals were so uncomplicated. She looked forward to spending two hours with simple creatures who had no pretenses and no secrets. Maybe she would stay late and pet the inhabitants of the cat room today.

That's where she was, cuddling a fuzzy orange kitten, when she heard the harmonica music start. Smiling, Kit put Puddy back with his sisters and followed the music. She found Mr. Morrison serenading a forlorn-looking bulldog.

"I've been thinking about what you told me," she said, "and I've decided you're partly wrong."

"Enlighten me," he said.

"Grownups can free themselves," Kit said, "but kids can't."

"Is that right?" Mr. Morrison stroked his beard.

"I can't leave home and as long as I'm there, my parents decide everything: if I can have a dog, if I go to college. I'm stuck with their decisions."

"You needn't leave home in order to free yourself. You just need to let go of your anger. Don't you see? Your parents can control whether or not you own a dog, but they can't keep you from loving the animals. No one can keep you out of college, if you want to go badly enough. When the doors are locked, girl, climb out a window."

It was nearly dark when she got home and the house was empty. She supposed Wayne had gone to the hospital after work. Her stomach growled as she went to the kitchen. She realized she was spoiled; Dorothy always had dinner started by the time Kit got home.

She was opening a can of stew when she heard Wayne's car in the driveway. A few moments later, he entered the kitchen.

"Hi, Wayne," Kit said. "I'm fixing us a bowl of stew. I just got here myself and . . ."

"I'm not hungry," Wayne said loudly.

Kit froze. She knew that tone of voice too well. Slowly, she turned to look at Wayne.

His eyes were red and he swayed slightly as he stood there.

Not now, Kit thought. Not with Dorothy in the hospital. She emptied the stew into a pan and turned on the burner. From the corner of her eye she watched Wayne open a cupboard, get out a glass and a bottle, and pour himself a drink.

"Are you going to the hospital tonight?" she asked.

"For what?"

"To visit Dorothy. I didn't go after school. I thought maybe you would go tonight." Actually, she had thought they would both go but she had no intention of going anywhere with Wayne now, not when he'd been drinking.

Wayne was silent. Surely, Kit thought, he remembers that she's in the hospital. He can't be that drunk, can he?

Finally, he answered. "I'm staying home," he said.

Just as well, Kit thought. He shouldn't be driving and he would only embarrass Dorothy if he showed up at the hospital this way. She would call her mother and explain. Dorothy wouldn't like it but she would agree it was better for Wayne to stay home.

Kit stirred the stew and opened a box of crackers.

"I need another drink," Wayne said. He held his glass toward Kit, as if he thought she would refill it for him.

She pretended she didn't see him. She ladled some stew into a bowl. "Sure you don't want some stew?" she said. "There's plenty."

"I said, I need another drink."

"So, get one."

"You get it for me."

"I'm not your waitress." She opened a drawer and took out a spoon.

"Get it for me."

"What happened to our agreement?" Kit said. "Yesterday you promised to be a better father. You said you wanted to get along with me, for Dorothy's sake."

Wayne blinked at her, scowling as if she were speaking French or German.

"If you really want to get along with me," Kit said, "you'd better not have another drink."

"Are you telling me I've had too much to drink?"

Kit hesitated. She knew how Wayne would react if she said *yes* but she was sick of lying. Wayne had a drinking problem. Maybe he wouldn't admit it but that didn't mean she had to pretend. She stepped toward him. "Yes," she said. "You've had too much to drink. Instead of getting you another one, I'll make you a pot of coffee."

Wayne pounded his fist on the table and bellowed. "Who do you think you are, telling me I've had too much?"

Kit knew there was no point saying anything else. She picked up her bowl of stew and carried it out of the kitchen. If he was going to sit there and drink, she certainly wasn't going to watch him.

She clicked on the television in the living room. She would eat her stew while she watched the six o'clock news. She'd had only two bites when Wayne appeared in front of the TV screen.

"You're acting too smart for your own good," he said.

"Wayne, please. I don't want to argue with you. Let's make a deal: I'll leave you alone and you leave me alone. How about it?" Kit forced herself to smile at him, hoping she could cajole him into a better mood.

"You've always acted too smart," he said. "Like you were the genius and I was the stupid one. Well, I'm not stupid."

"I never said you were."

"I can tell what you're thinking. Just because you get As on your report cards, you think other people are stupid."

Kit ate another spoonful of stew. "Why do you like to drink?" she asked.

The question caught Wayne off guard. "Huh?" he said.

"Why do you drink? Does it make you feel happy?"

He stared at her, his mouth hanging slightly open.

"I'm just curious," Kit went on. "You never seem happy when you're drinking so I just wondered why you do it."

"It makes me forget my problems."

"It doesn't make them go away, though. When you sober up, the problems are still there, big as ever. Maybe bigger."

Wayne pointed a finger at her. Kit saw that his hand was shaking. "There," he said. "That's what I mean. You always talk so smart and make me seem stupid."

Why did he keep insisting that she thought he was stupid? She had never said that, to him or anyone else. She wondered if he thought of himself that way. Maybe that was the real problem. And maybe the time had come for her to tell him exactly what she thought. He was angry at her anyway. Maybe it was time to bring everything out in the open.

"Wayne," she said, "you are an alcoholic."

"No, I'm not. I can handle my . . ."

"Yes, you are," she said firmly. "But you can change, if you want to. Lots of people have a drinking problem. And do you know what they do? If they're smart, they admit it. They admit it and then they join Alcoholics Anonymous or they go to a treatment center. They get help. They change."

Wayne turned and walked away from her, back to the kitchen.

Kit followed him. "I know you don't want to hear this," she said, "but I have to say it. The main reason I've never felt close to you, and never wanted you to be my father, is because of how you act when you're drunk."

"I'm not drunk!"

"Denying the truth won't change it. I've seen you this way too many times."

"You . . ."

Kit rushed on, the words racing forward like a forest fire out of control. "When you aren't drinking, we get along OK. At the hospital yesterday, when we were waiting, I felt real close to you. Why do you have to spoil it all by getting drunk again?"

"I'm not drunk. Quit saying that."

"Why can't you just admit the truth? Instead, you always pretend you aren't drunk and Dorothy pretends, too. Well, I'm sorry but I can't go along with your lie any longer."

"Listen to the little thief talk about honesty!"

The word *thief* was cold water on the flame of Kit's outrage. She slumped against the refrigerator.

Wayne glared at her. "You think you know all about it," he said. "Well, you don't know anything. You hear me? You don't know anything." He took a step toward her, swaying slightly. He spoke deliberately, as if choosing each word from a thesaurus. "You—are—nothing—but—an—animal."

Always in the past when he had called her an animal, it had infuriated her. This time, when she heard the word animal, she thought of all the animals she had worked with at The Humane Society. She thought of wagging tails and purring kittens, of caged puppies who licked her fingers, delighted to see her. She thought of Lady, with the love light shining in her eyes.

"You're an animal," Wayne repeated.

"Thank you," Kit said.

Wayne looked astonished. "I called you an animal."

"I know. It's the nicest compliment you could give me." She smiled sweetly at him. For the first time in her life, Kit felt in charge when Wayne was drinking. She couldn't make him stop but she would control her own reactions. He had lost his power over her.

"But . . . you . . ." Wayne sputtered.

She went to the phone and dialed Tracy's number. "Could I stay with you tonight?" she said.

Kit packed quickly. When she came downstairs, Wayne still stood exactly where she had left him. As she opened the front door, Kit almost felt sorry for him. "Goodnight," she said. "I'll be at Tracy's house."

Wayne did not respond.

CHAPTER

16

MRS. Shelburn drove Kit to the hospital, insisting that Kit should visit her mother. "Tracy and I will wait for you in the lobby," she said. "Take your time."

Kit was grateful. It was bad enough for Dorothy to learn that Wayne was on another binge; she knew it would be even worse to get the news with other people present.

When Kit walked into the room alone, she saw instant fear in Dorothy's eyes.

"Where's Wayne?" Dorothy asked.

Kit sat beside her mother's bed. "He's drunk again," she said.

The look of concern turned to dismay. Dorothy was quiet for several seconds. Then she said, "When you get home, go in our bedroom and get the car keys. After he falls alseep, try to get his wallet, too. Hide them someplace where he can't find them."

"I'm not going home. I'm staying at Tracy's. Mrs. Shelburn is waiting for me downstairs."

"But we can't let him . . ." Dorothy stopped. "Yes," she said. "It's better for you to be with the Shelburns."

She doesn't need this, Kit thought. Wayne should be the strong one now. She shouldn't have to worry about anything except getting well.

"Maybe the doctor will discharge me early," Dorothy said.

"So you can go home and wait on him?" Kit said. "That's the most disgusting thing I ever heard."

"When he's sick like this," Dorothy said softly, "I need to be there."

"You've had major surgery. He should be taking care of you."

Dorothy went on as if she didn't hear. "I'll need to call his boss in the morning," she said.

"If you didn't cover up for him," Kit said, "maybe he would be forced to admit he has a problem. Maybe he would do something about it."

"I can't let him lose his job. I have to call his boss."

Kit felt sad for her mother but she didn't argue. If Dorothy wanted to stay in her cage, there was nothing Kit could do about it.

Later that night, Kit and Tracy made popcorn and read fashion magazines. Then Tracy gave part of her sibling rivalry speech for Kit.

Sharon Shocker announced, "EINSTEIN BRAIN TRANSPLANT REVEALED! GIRL GENIUS GETS A+ ON SPEECH."

"It *is* a school night," Mrs. Shelburn reminded them, "and you'll be up late tomorrow night, with your dress rehearsal."

Kit and Tracy promised her that they would go right to sleep, with no talking.

"That will be an historic first," Mrs. Shelburn replied.

Half an hour later, Tracy whispered, "I have to ask you something personal." Her voice, from the other twin bed, was so soft that Kit had to strain to hear the words.

"Go ahead."

"Do you have a boyfriend?"

"Oh, sure," Kit said. "Several dozen."

"I'm serious."

"If I had a boyfriend, don't you think you would know about him?"

"Would I?" Tracy sounded wistful.

Kit realized that this wasn't a joke question. "What are you getting at?" she asked.

"You've been so secretive lately. I feel like you're hiding something from me and I've tried to figure out what it could be and the only thing that seems to make sense is that you've found someone else you want to be with, someone you like better than me."

"Oh, Tracy."

"Let me finish," Tracy said. "If you *do* have a boyfriend, it's OK. I understand. You don't have to tell me who it is; I just want to know if that's what's going on. Is it?"

"No. I do not have a boyfriend."

"Oh."

"And I can't imagine ever finding anyone, male or female, that I'd like better than you. Even when I do have a boyfriend, if I ever do, it won't mean that we have to stop being friends."

There was such a long silence that Kit thought Tracy had fallen asleep. Through the bedroom window, Kit watched the crescent moon play peek-a-boo with the clouds.

Tracy whispered again. "My birthday party. The Good Citizen Award. Something is wrong, Kit. What is it?"

For a moment, Kit was tempted to tell her. Here in the dark, snuggled deep in their beds, Kit and Tracy had divulged dozens of secrets in the past. They had confided their crushes on various boys, and their fears that they were ugly, and their dreams for the future. They had confessed problems, both real and imagined, and had learned that talking about a fear sometimes makes it less threatening. Over the years, they had cemented their friendship by sharing their worries as well as their fun.

But those worries were different from Kit's current problem. Never before had Kit faced a predicament that was entirely her own fault. It was one thing to complain when Wayne did something she didn't like or to confide that she thought a certain boy was cute. It was quite another to admit that she had broken the law. TRIK Club members were honest.

Kit said nothing. Her twenty required hours at The Humane Society were nearly finished. The shoplifting would eventually be erased from her record. She saw no reason to tell Tracy now.

"I know you aren't asleep," Tracy said. "I can tell by your breathing."

"I told you before," Kit said, her voice sounding sharper than she intended, "I don't have any problem."

Tracy did not reply.

The next morning, Mrs. Shelburn insisted that Kit stay with

them until Dorothy was released from the hospital. "You can borrow anything you need from Tracy," she said. "There's no reason at all for you to go back home."

Kit gratefully accepted the offer.

That night when they went to bed, Tracy turned out the light, said, "Goodnight," and that was it. No whispered conversation. No giggling. No sharing of secrets. It was the first time that they had spent the night together without any talk in the dark before they fell asleep. Kit missed it but she could think of nothing to say.

When Kit got to the hospital after school the next day, Dorothy was not in her room. Kit looked in the bathroom and in the hallway. Finally, she inquired at the nurse's station.

"She's downstairs," the nurse said. "In Emergency."

"Emergency?" Kit cried. "What happened? She was supposed to go home tomorrow."

"Nothing happened to her," the nurse said. "She's still scheduled to be released tomorrow. Are you her daughter?"

"Yes."

"Then it wasn't you. She was afraid it was you." Seeing the blank look on Kit's face, the nurse went on, "We got a call from Emergency, saying that a member of Mrs. Gillette's family was being admitted. That's all I know."

Kit didn't wait for the elevator. She ran down the stairs and followed the signs to the emergency area.

She found Dorothy sitting alone in the waiting room, crying. She wore her yellow terrycloth bathrobe and her slippers. "Wayne had an accident," Dorothy explained. "He went off the road and ran into a light post. He wasn't wearing a seat belt and he was thrown out of the car." She blew her nose.

"How bad is it?" Kit asked.

"Concussion. Probably a skull fracture. Broken left arm. Maybe internal injuries."

He was drunk, Kit thought. Usually his binges lasted three or four days, which meant he would be at his worst about now.

"There was a police officer here a little while ago," Dorothy said. "Wayne's been ticketed for driving while intoxicated."

Kit wasn't surprised. It was bound to happen, sooner or later.

"We're lucky he didn't kill anybody," Dorothy said. Her face was pale and when she wiped her eyes, Kit noticed that her hands shook.

"Are you OK?" Kit asked. "Shouldn't you go back to bed?"

Dorothy wilted against the chair. "I'm tired," she admitted. "I've been so worried. Ever since you said you were staying with the Shelburns, I've had the feeling that Wayne would get into trouble. Always before when he was like this, I was there. I took care of him. I always hid the car keys, so he couldn't drive."

Kit felt a rush of sympathy for Dorothy. She could only guess how hard Wayne's binges must be on her mother.

"You were right," Dorothy said. "He does have a drinking problem and if he lives through this, I'm going to insist that he get some help. I should have done it years ago, but each time I hoped he had learned his lesson. Each time, I thought it wouldn't happen again. And you know how stubborn Wayne is."

Kit helped Dorothy back to her own room and into bed. She stayed at the hospital until six o'clock. Then, after stopping at the small florist shop next to the hospital, she rushed back to school. She didn't take time to eat dinner.

It was opening night of the play and she didn't want to be late. Kit sat in the front row, cradling six red roses. She planned to give them to Tracy during the curtain call.

The auditorium was full. Kit knew her posters had helped. She had put them in store windows all over town.

As she waited for the curtains to open, she read the program. When she saw, "Kennedy School presents *The Member of the Wedding* by Carson McCullers, starring Marcia Homer as Frankie," she felt a sharp twinge of longing but she no longer hoped that Marcia would forget her lines. Everyone had worked too hard to make the play a success. She wanted it to be perfect.

It was electrifying.

Marcia was magnificent. She was no longer Marcia Homer. Even to Kit, who knew her well, she was transformed. She was Frankie.

At the end, Kit applauded until her hands stung. During the second curtain call, she went forward. Impulsively, she gave only three of the roses to Tracy; she gave the other three to Marcia.

Afterwards, backstage, Marcia thanked her. "And I also want to thank you for helping me get Pansy. It's super to have a dog again. She sleeps in my room. She's always there when I get home and she thinks I'm wonderful." Marcia looked down. "I never quite measure up to my parents' expectations. I try, but I'm not as smart as they want me to be or as good looking. Pansy doesn't care; she thinks I'm fine just the way I am."

138

Kit was incredulous. From what she had seen, Marcia's parents both thought their daughter was wonderful. How could Marcia not know that?

Before Kit could say so, other people gathered around Marcia, telling her how good she was in the play. Kit listened as Marcia accepted their praise gracefully. Now that she had a reason to brag, Marcia sounded downright modest.

She needed this, Kit realized, and then wondered if Miss Fenton knew that when she picked the cast.

CHAPTER
17

ONE week. That's all the time Kit had left to prepare her final speech. She couldn't put it off any longer.

"What's your cousin's phone number?" she asked Tracy. "I want to interview Glorie for my shoplifting speech."

"It'll be an expensive call," Tracy said. "She and her family are living in London this year."

Kit groaned. She had counted on Glorie to be her original research. Now what was she going to do? She had plenty of library references for her speech but Miss Fenton required at least one personal interview.

Reluctantly, Kit telephoned Pierre's and asked to speak to Hannah Rydecker. While she waited, she took deep breaths, trying to calm herself.

When Mrs. Rydecker answered, Kit told her who she was

and what she wanted. She spoke fast, anxious to get it over with. She half expected Mrs. Rydecker to hang up on her. Why would the security guard want to spend time talking to Kit?

"I'll be glad to meet with you," Mrs. Rydecker said, when Kit had finished her explanation. "Can you come tomorrow at four?"

"Yes."

"Do you remember where my office is?"

"Yes." Do I remember? I will never in my whole life forget where your office is.

The next day, Kit almost chickened out. When it came time to actually walk into Pierre's and go to the security office, she wasn't sure she could go through with it. She had to walk past the pianist. She had to walk through the jewelry department. The memories of that night were so strong that for a moment she even imagined she saw Marcia and Mr. Homer.

Mrs. Rydecker was waiting for her. She asked what had happened when Kit met with the Juvenile Court Committee and Kit told her about The Humane Society.

Then Kit got out the list of questions she wanted to ask and Mrs. Rydecker talked for half an hour about her job. She told Kit that shoplifting costs the store thousands of dollars every year.

"Of course, the store passes those costs on to the consumer," she said. "Every time you or I buy something, we pay more for it, to help offset the cost of stolen merchandise."

By the time the interview ended, Kit had scribbled two pages of notes on her tablet. She knew she had plenty of solid information for her speech.

"Thanks for your help," she said, as she prepared to leave.

"I hope I see you again," Mrs. Rydecker said. Then she added, "But not with a badge in my hand."

"No badge," Kit vowed. "Not ever again."

As Kit left Pierre's, she gave a huge sigh of relief. After dreading the interview all day, it had turned out to be a breeze.

If she had not done it, she would have felt uneasy in Pierre's, afraid she would see Hannah Rydecker again.

She wasn't afraid anymore.

All she had to do now was get through her final speech. After that, if she never heard the word "shoplifting" again, it would be fine with her. Her twenty hours of time at The Humane Society were history; her debt to society was paid. She had managed to keep the whole affair a secret. As soon as her speech was finished, Kit could forget that it ever happened. Forget the night in Pierre's; forget the court committee; forget that she had ever stolen a gold bracelet.

On the second day of the final speeches, Miss Fenton called on Kit. Kit had practiced her speech over and over the night before. She was prepared and she wanted to get it over with but she still dreaded it. She jumped when Miss Fenton called her name and when she faced the class and announced her topic, she began trembling.

Despite her anxiety, she managed to remember what she had rehearsed. She used all of the statistics that Mrs. Rydecker had given her and then ended her speech by telling the class, "If you're caught shoplifting, your parents are notified, and the police come, and the juvenile court decides your punishment. It's stupid to take such a chance."

And that's when Arthur challenged her. That's when he and Phil said it's easy to shoplift. That's when Miss Fenton said,

"Do you want to defend your speech, Kit? This minute is passing."

As Kit stood with all eyes on her, the rest of that line from the play came back to her. ". . . this minute is passing. And it will never come again. Never in all the world. When it is gone, it is gone. No power on earth could bring it back again."

She realized that if she sat down now, Tracy would ask her why she didn't defend her speech and Kit would have no answer. The barrier between them, built of secrecy and lies, would grow stronger. She would have to keep on hiding what she had done and she would always worry that Tracy might somehow find out about it.

If she told the truth, everyone would know what she had done but she would never again have to worry that her secret would come out. She could prove Arthur wrong and she might prevent someone else from making the silly, tragic mistake that she had made. She could eliminate, once and for all, the fence that separated her from Tracy.

Right then, in that singular, fleeting moment, Kit knew she had a chance to free herself.

Kit threw back her shoulders, turned, and marched to the front of the room.

"Yes," she said. "I want to defend my speech."

Miss Fenton nodded her approval.

Kit faced the class and began.

"Three months ago," she said, "I stole a bracelet from Pierre's." Someone gasped.

Except for the part about Wayne, Kit told the whole story. Every detail. How she'd been upset, how she put the bracelet in her pocket, and how she got caught. When she told how scared she was and how her mother cried, the room was still as a tomb; no papers rustled, no one shifted in their seat, no one coughed or whispered.

"I tried to hide what I did," she said. "I was so ashamed that I didn't even tell my best friend. I missed her birthday party because I had to appear that night before the Juvenile Court Committee—and I didn't tell her why I couldn't go to the party. I was afraid that if she found out, she wouldn't like me anymore."

She glanced at Tracy. Tracy looked like she was going to cry.

"Sure," Kit continued, "I didn't go to jail. But I had to pay three hundred dollars and I had to do twenty hours of community service work. Worst of all, I had to live with a terrible secret. I told lies to keep people from finding out what I'd done and then I had to tell more lies to cover up the first ones. Through it all, I felt like scum. I regretted what I had done and I hated pretending all the time but it was too late. Once I took the bracelet and got caught, I couldn't go back."

She pointed to Arthur. "Maybe your friend hasn't been caught. Maybe he'll never be caught. But he'll never have any self-respect, either."

Arthur did not respond.

"I quoted statistics," Kit said, "but I speak from experience, too." Her voice rang with conviction. "Shoplifting is a crime. When you're caught, you're a criminal and that's how the police treat you."

Tears came to Kit's eyes. Talking about her experience this way was like living it over again. "If you are ever tempted to shoplift," she said, "stop and think about me. Think what it would be like for you if you got caught. I've been there and I can tell you, it isn't any fun." She paused. No one moved. "Please," she said, "obey the law. Don't shoplift."

Once again, she nodded at Miss Fenton, to indicate she was finished. Before she could take her seat, something happened that had never happened in speech class before. The students applauded. Two boys whistled. And then Tracy jumped to her feet, still clapping, and the rest of the class followed. Only Arthur and Phil, looking uneasy, remained seated.

Kit got her standing ovation.

She also got the only *A* grade that Miss Fenton gave that year. "It took courage," Miss Fenton wrote on Kit's grade slip. "It did what all great speeches do—it affected the audience emotionally."

After class, Tracy said, "You should have told me. You don't know how worried I was. I imagined all sorts of terrible things. I even thought you might have cancer or AIDS."

Kit's mouth dropped open. "Why would you think that?" she said. "I'm never sick."

"What was I supposed to think? I knew something was wrong and I knew it must be terrible or else you would tell me. So I figured out the worst possible secret I could think of." Tracy's eyes filled with tears. "I was so scared for you," she said.

"Oh, Tracy." Kit threw her arms around Tracy and hugged her. "I'm sorry I didn't tell you, but I was so ashamed."

"You made a big mistake. That doesn't mean you're a rotten person. At least you learned from your mistake; you won't do it again."

Kit wondered if Wayne would learn from his mistake, too.

The doctors said he would recover from his injuries and, after a week in the hospital, he was allowed to go home.

His arm was still in a cast on the day he went to traffic court. Drunk driving is a serious offense. Besides a stiff fine, Wayne lost his driver's license for two weeks and was warned that he would lose it permanently if he got caught driving while intoxicated again.

Kit got home from school shortly after Wayne and Dorothy returned from court. As she opened the front door, she heard Dorothy say, "You can't go on this way, Wayne. You might have killed someone. You might have killed yourself."

"I shouldn't have been driving," Wayne admitted.

"You shouldn't have been drinking," Dorothy said.

"I just had a little too much that night. You were in the hospital and I was lonely."

"No," Dorothy said. "It wasn't just that night. Every time you take a drink, you end up having too much."

"It won't happen again," Wayne said. "I promise."

Kit joined them in the kitchen as Dorothy said, "You've promised before. This time I want you to do more than promise."

"I'm not going to some counselor, if that's what you mean," Wayne said. "I can handle my own problems."

"No," Dorothy said firmly. "You can't."

"She's right," Kit said.

"You stay out of this," Wayne said. "It doesn't concern you."

"Yes, it does," Kit said.

Wayne started to protest but Kit held up her hand and continued. "I want to tell you something. The night I took the

146

bracelet, I did it because you were drunk. I came home unhappy but I had planned to take a bath and read. When you were drunk and you yelled at me, I ran out of the house and went to the mall."

Wayne looked as if she'd slapped him in the face.

"I'm not justifying what I did," Kit said. "It was wrong and I admit it. But I'm telling you that your drinking problem is a problem for all of us. Most of the time you're a decent guy but when you're drunk, I can't stand you."

Dorothy said, "She doesn't mean . . ." and then stopped. "That's right," she said.

Kit continued. "The other day you wondered what you have done wrong as a father. Well, I'll tell you. You drink too much."

She left the kitchen then. She'd had her say. The rest was up to Wayne.

Mr. Morrison was right about humans and their problems. Dorothy had freed herself from her fear of standing up to Wayne. Now Wayne would have to free himself from his drinking.

And me? What about my cages? She remembered how frustrated and angry she used to feel, how she resented what Wayne and Dorothy did.

I'm not angry anymore, she realized. I still can't control what they do but they can't control how I feel. Nobody can. I'm able to choose how I act, what I say and do. I can be the kind of person I want to be, no matter what Dorothy and Wayne do.

I'm already free. And I'll never be caged again.

* * *

147

On the evening of the last day of school, Kit and Dorothy went to the awards night ceremony.

"I feel like I should go, too," Wayne said, as they prepared to leave. "But I don't want to miss my A.A. meeting."

"I would much rather have you go to A.A.," Kit said.

"So would I," Dorothy said.

Kit didn't know what else had been said that day in the kitchen. She knew only that the very next night, Wayne had attended his first Alcoholics Anonymous meeting. He'd been to two more meetings since.

Kit and Dorothy sat with the Shelburns. When the Good Citizen Award was presented, Tracy nudged Kit and whispered, "I still think you should have had that one."

Kit smiled at her. It was good to know that Tracy felt that way even now, when she knew why Kit began going to The Humane Society.

The last award was the Ninth Grade Scholarship. Before it was presented, the school band played a Souza march. While she listened, Kit read about the scholarship in the program. It explained that the scholarship money was invested and the interest it earned would compound. In three years, when the recipient was ready to start college, the scholarship would cover tuition, room and board, and books for the first two years.

Even though she had blown her chance for the scholarship, Kit was determined she would still go to college. As soon as she finished paying her debt to Wayne, she would save her baby-sitting money for college. Soon she'd be old enough to get a part-time job. She would study hard and keep her grades up and maybe there would be other scholarships, other opportunities. As Mr. Morrison said, if the doors were locked, she would climb out a window.

One way or another, she would get to college. She had to, because for the first time in her life, she knew what she wanted to be.

When the band finished, Miss Fenton stood up to announce the winner of the Ninth Grade Scholarship.

She began by saying that the winner had maintained excellent grades all year. "She also participated in extracurricular activities, such as the school play," Miss Fenton said.

"Oh, no," Tracy whispered. "Not Marcia. She doesn't need a scholarship."

"Shhh," said Mrs. Shelburn.

"Most of all," Miss Fenton said, "she has displayed courage and leadership ability. It is my privilege to present the Ninth Grade Scholarship to Kit Hathaway."

Tracy let out a whoop.

Dorothy gasped. "Kit," she said, "that's you!"

Kit walked forward in a daze. All she could think was, I'm going to college. It doesn't matter what Wayne thinks; I'm going to college.

As Miss Fenton handed her the award she said, "We'd like you to say a few words about your plans for a college career." Her eyes twinkled as she added, in a whisper, "One last speech."

Kit stood tall in front of the microphone and thanked the school for the award. "After I finish college," she said, "I want to go on to veterinary school. I plan to spend my life working with animals."

As Kit returned to her seat, Harriet Headline said, "FUTURE

VETERINARIAN WINS PRESTIGIOUS SCHOLARSHIP. PRESIDENT AND CONGRESS WIRE CONGRATULATIONS. NEW NATIONAL HOLIDAY DECLARED!"

Dorothy's face glowed with excitement. Kit didn't remember ever seeing her mother look so happy. She was luminous, her eyes shining. And then Kit realized what she saw.

Love light. She saw love light in Dorothy's eyes. Had it always been there? Had she failed to notice before because her own mind was filled with resentment? She could almost hear harmonica music in the background.

"I am so proud of you," Dorothy said. "So very proud."

"Thanks," Kit said, as she squeezed Dorothy's hand. "Thanks, Mom."

Peg Kehret lives in a log house in the woods near Mount Rainier National Park in Washington State. She and her husband, Carl, have two grown children and four grandchildren.

Peg's popular books often appear on recommended lists from the International Reading Association and the American Library Association. They are regularly nominated for young readers' awards, which she has won many times. She has written over thirty books.

An animal lover and Humane Society volunteer, Peg also likes to read, pump her player piano, and watch baseball.